RATCHET

Billie Dureya Shell

RATCHET

Copyright © 2020

All rights reserved to Billie Dureyea Shell.

No part of this publication may be reproduced, distributed or transmitted in any form or by any means, including photocopying, or other electronic or mechanical methods, without the prior written permission of the publisher, except in the case of brief quotations embodied in critical reviews and certain noncommercial uses permitted by copyright law. Any references to historical events, real people or real places are used factiously. Names, characters, and places are products of the authors imagination.

Front Cover Image By grafic designer Billie Dureyea Shell & Kenny Writes

First Printing Edition 2020

This book is dedicated to:

My uncle Wo ody I love you Unc this one is 4
you........ Tell Antie Marie and my cousin
I love them

Team Shell

Acknowledgement

2020 has been a good year 4 me and my family And that's all becuz our father above so once again I want 2 give thank 2 God for this gift I am so grateful for him giving me away 2 provide 4 my family in my house we will alwayz put you first.

To my mother Mclessie Shell you taught me so much and you loved me NO MATTER WHAT I love you

so much momma.... What's up with some

bake chicken □LOL 😁😂□.

To my little sister Glenda I love you and miss you blackie get at ur big brother Lil Sis.

To my Wife Shatoya Shell you get on my damn nerves ☐♂ but I wouldnt trade you 4 anything In the world I Iove ❤ you more then words can ever express.

To all my children ☐☐☐ I love y'all Jazmine, Ant'Tuan, Davon, Anthony, David, Lil Dureyea, Alura, Queen Diavion, Cameron, Preniece, Shaniece and Tajh I love u all and I'll 4ever have ur back you all give me a reason 2 smile... to my cousin Zane RIP nigga I miss u more then anyone will ever no, your always remembered love you bro.

To my cousin Ty I miss you thank 4 looking out 4 me and Zane you played a big part in my life and I always looked up to you l love you... Uncle Woody I miss you and love you, you no your my favorite uncle....

To my nigga Jamal love you, my brothers Lawrence and fred thank 4 showing me the game I love yall 4 that.

To my oldest sister Nedra love you thank you 4 always having my back. to my family uncles anties cousins etc.. I love y'all even those of you that act funny as fuck To my dark side niggas y'all no what it is YAAH GANG........

Now to all my readers and fans I love you thanks for reading I hope u enjoy this book as much as I enjoy writing them with this Corona Virus 19 shit there ain't shit to do but write so I'm on my shit with that being said y'all be safe cover your face and love each other life is short so love the ones that really love you I'm gone enjoy the book.

AND STAY SAFE

Author

Billie Dureyea Shell

Ratchet

Chapter 1

DEFINITION OF INSANITY

Most of the chicks I fuck with say I'm selfish and cold-hearted. That's not true; oi'p I just get put in bad situations that make me look like the bad guy. For instance, right now, I'm locked in a bathroom with my girl's cousin. This wasn't my plan, and hell, I didn't even like this girl before she busted into the bathroom and started kissing me. Kissing lead to some head and of course I wasn't gonna turn down no pussy. So now, instead of being downstairs with my girl's family, eating Christmas dinner, I was upstairs in the bathroom, fucking her cousin. Somebody might look at this and say I'm a dog ass nigga, but she came on to me. There was nothing I could do about it now since I was balls deep in my girl's cousin. I'm sorry that I had her bent over the sink in this tiny ass bathroom. I should have turned her down, but my sex drive was too high for that. I always found myself in these dumb ass positions, and now all I wanted to do was nut and get the fuck out of here. A few knocks on the door stopped me in mid stroke. "Somebody in there? Is the door stuck again?" When I saw the door knob twist, my heart damn near burst out of my chest. "Naw, I'm in here." I yelled, trying to keep whoever it was away as I put my foot near the door to keep them from busting in. They didn't want to see this, and if they did open the door, even death wasn't gonna save me from the shit that would happen. My girl Serena was gonna beat me and this bitch's ass if she found out about this. Maybe I should have thought of that before, too, but my dick didn't have a conscience. All he saw was ass, titties, and a mouth saying 'fuck me', and he was ready to go. If I made it out of this, I promised myself I was going to church on Sunday. I said a quick prayer, but I had a feeling that with my dick deep in some pussy, God probably wasn't trying to hear what the fuck I had to say. Nevertheless, I prayed anyway, with my hands on Tanya's hips instead of folded, 'cuz I was still too afraid to move or even fucking breath. Thank God Tanya had locked the door or I woulda already been caught red-handed with my dick in the cookie jar. "Are you okay, then? Been in here for a minute." I heard some voice that I didn't recognize, but hell, it was Christmas with a house full of my girl's people milling around. I didn't know more than half of the people here. "Yeah, okay, just not feeling too good." My voice wavered as I lied. Tanya started pushing her pussy back on me, obviously not caring that we were about to get caught. With every second that went by, she got wetter, as if this sneaking shit turned her on. This girl was a dare devil; instead of waiting until things were clear, she was ready to get it back poppin. "Aight," whoever it was said and I heard them walk away. We went back to what we were doing but that had been close...too close.

Chapter 2

The bathroom was now like a private hotel. All I needed was ten minutes and I would be done with Tanya, but with how good her pussy felt, it would be even less than that if she kept tightening her muscles around me. No wonder this bitch had so many kids: her shit was too good, and here I was falling for the bullshit in the damn bathroom with my pants on the floor and her skirt up to her waist. I tried to concentrate and hurry things up, but her moans and screams kept throwing me off. Her head hit the door, and her moans bounced off the walls of the bathroom. Like she didn't know we weren't supposed to be fucking and there weren't almost fifty people downstairs. I'd already stuffed her panties in her mouth to shut her up, but it still didn't help. "Shut up!" I whispered to her. The last thing we needed was somebody to hear us. Good dick like mine had this effect on chicks. Normally, I would have wanted to hear my name screamed while I was plowing dick, but today we needed to be quiet. I pumped into her from behind, and from the mirror I could see that her face frowned and scrunched up as I dug deeper inside her. That shit turned me on, and my dick felt like a drill sinking into her wetness, but we still had a problem. The face I was staring at wasn't my girl Serena, but the face of her cousin Tanya. I'd known Tanya wanted me – all the winking and brushing of her ass and titties on me wasn't innocent, but I'd ignored that shit. Now I was dick deep inside her, though, and it was too late to be wrong now. "Fuck, Landis. Your dick is so good." Tanya told me what I already knew, and that only made me work harder. I pumped faster...harder...until the knocks came. More knocks. "Is somebody in here?" I stopped breathing again, but my dick was already spitting hot cum. I pulled out, damn near falling in the bathtub. I caught myself pulling on the towel bar for leverage before I crashed in the tub and made more noise. "Yeah, my stomach just a little messed up. I'll be out." My voice was between a scream and a moan as I grabbed a towel to stop my seeds from pumping out on the floor but I was too late. My dick didn't have a good aim when it was cuming. It looked like a massacre of frosting with some getting on the floor and every-damn-where else, but I just didn't want it inside Tanya. Of course, when she'd come in the bathroom, she hadn't had a condom and neither had I, but that never stopped me from getting no pussy. "Fuck." The word slipped from my mouth when some of my nut got on my jeans. "You okay?" The voice asked, and there was more shuffling of the door knob as Tanya pulled down her skirt. The smirk on her face said it all...

Chapter 3

Tonya loved this shit. "Yeah, I'm good. Be right out." I flushed the toilet and Tanya turned on the faucet, but none of that would save us from walking out this door. "Aight, baby. Probably Aunt Maureen's greens. It's pepto under the sink." I recognized the voice, Serena's mom. That was the last person I needed to see this. Only if I could be faithful, but how do you stay with one chick at a time? In my twenty-seven years, I haven't been able to figure it out. I tried being a lame ass nigga, settling down, and being with one, but it never works. Bitches are too crazy. So I keep hoes in rotation, but can't tell you why. That's just the way I am.

Holidays are my time. Starting at Christmas, I decide who I'm gonna fuck with for the winter, but it's never just one chick. I always have several, with some possible waiting in the wings. Like right now – it's Christmas and I'm at my main chick's house chilling with her family, but later on I had plans to dip with somebody else. I had to keep my options open. Now my dick went down and I cleaned up my spilled cum with my mind working overtime. I had to get out of this bathroom without anybody seeing, then get out of the house and clear my mind. But Tanya looked like a kid in a candy store. She was happy: this was some kind of sick shit. And it seemed like she'd planned for it to happen like this. "I see why Serena is in love with yo ass." She washed her hands like this was nothing. "Guess she won't mind if we share," she licked her dick-sucking lips, slowly, while she showed off how fat and juicy they were. Almost like she wanted to go for round two. I didn't have time to ask her what she meant by 'share'. I didn't have no intention of fucking her again; hell, that was if I still had my dick after today. I was ready to tell her I was going out first, but she beat me to it. She was out of the bathroom and closing the door behind her before I could speak. I waited to hear somebody's voice with my head to the door. Tanya's heels clicking and then Serena's Mom screaming. My chest was pounding, and my stomach turned as I thought about maybe jumping out the bathroom window to get away. I listened to what was being said, thinking fast about how I was going to get the fuck out of here. No way could I face my girl, her family, and her cousin who I'd just fucked. All of this on Christmas, right before tax time. How could I be so fucking stupid?

Chapter 4

The screaming stopped and turned into laughter. That was Serena's mom, Ms. Pettis, alright. She was naturally loud, and could either be happy or upset, but you often couldn't tell the difference. The screaming I'd heard was just Serena's mom laughing about something on the TV. After a minute that stopped, and I heard nothing but the TVs and people talking. "Fuck, Landis." I looked myself over in the mirror again. "Why you gotta be so irresistible to these hoes?" I asked, but I already knew the answer. I could see why bitches couldn't keep their hands off me. My hazel eyes made it hard, and my brown cocoa skin made me look like I was from the Middle East or something. But most of all, my dick always had bitches bragging to their friends. If only they knew, talking to other females about my dick game only made them want a piece. Minutes went by and still nothing, so I figured she must have gotten away without someone seeing her. A woman coming out of the bathroom where I'd just been locked in should have been sure to bring screams, cursing, and some type of fight. When I didn't hear that, I knew it was clear, but getting out of the bathroom was only the first step. I was ready to leave this house before I had a damn heart attack. My stomach really was sick now doing flip flops with every second I stayed in the bathroom. My nerves kicked in but to be a dog you had to have nerves of steel. Maybe I was getting older and I couldn't keep up lies like I'd used to. Having to sit around here with the smell of Tanya on my dick, and Serena and her family in my face, was gonna fuck my stomach up for real. I splashed water on my face, formulating a lie. "My stomach's fucked up. I'm gonna head home." I repeated the lie, trying to look pitiful. It looked believable, as I threw more water on my face and smoothed down my hair. I wiped up the bathroom as best as I could. Spraying almost the whole can of air freshener and cracking the window. The towel with my nut on it went in the trash, and I cleaned my pants off, preparing for Serena's laser eyes. She always caught shit that I thought no one could see. Deep breaths, and I twisted the door knob, leaving the small room where I'd fucked my Serena's cousin and shot cum all over the floor. Down the steps, everyone was talking and I listened to their words. From football to the food, there were a dozen conversations, but luckily, none of them were about me. "Where you go, Landis? Game's on, man." That was Serena's step-father. His salt and pepper bearded face smiled at me but if only he knew what I'd been doing upstairs in his bathroom, he wouldn't be so happy. "Aww man. My stomach, man. I gotta go home." I lied, a sick puppy-dog look on my face. Serena came from nowhere, touching me from behind and making me jump. "What's wrong, baby? My momma said you was in the bathroom sick?" Her eyes looked like she knew the truth, brown and piercing right through me, but I continued the lie. "Yeah, I don't know what it is. But Imma go home." She knew me better than anybody, and I prayed she bought it, until Tanya's hoe ass showed up. "You know you could lay down here." Tanya laughed, and Serena glared at the bitch. They were cousins, but they didn't like each other. And now as Serena rolled her eyes at Tanya, I realized what was going on; she'd used me to get back at her cousin and I was dumb enough to fall for it. "Why is that bitch all in my business?" Serna hissed under her breath and I shrugged, pretending not to know as the crowded living room of friends, family, and kids walked back and forth past us. I knew I was supposed to be playing sick, but I was starting to feel queasy for real. This shit wasn't right. "Babe, I gotta go. I'm gonna see you at home." She'd driven her car and I'd driven mine. I moved towards the door, but she grabbed her coat, too. "Okay, I'll walk you out." Fuck, I just wanted to hop in the car and leave. Waving bye to everybody, I saw that Tanya and her boyfriend were in the corner talking. His face was in a frown and his eyes were on me. Something about that didn't make me feel any better.

"Alright, son-in-law. See you later." Tanya's mom came over to give me a hug. I hated when she called me that shit like me and Serena were married but I never said anything. I slipped out the door headed to my car, but Serena was right on my heels like a dog following their master. "You think you coming down with something? Like a cold, maybe?" Serena wouldn't let this shit go. But that was her, being caring, but it was too bad I wasn't that type of nigga. I did shit my way and sometimes that meant I wasn't completely faithful. It made it hard to be the way I was with her being so nice. She was a good woman, but that didn't mean shit to me. All I wanted was the money. "Naw, man, I'm cool. Just too many damn people in there knocking on the door while I'm trying to take a shit." I was getting mad now. Why did she have to ask so many questions? "Aight, then. I guess I'll just see you at home. What's wrong, why are you getting so mad?" She blocked the door to the car, her eyes piercing through me and trying to figure out what was wrong with me. "Nothing, man. I just wanna go home before I shit on myself." I rubbed my stomach, but she wasn't looking at me anymore. She was looking behind me. "Hey, motherfucka. Let me holla at you." Turning around, I saw it was Tanya's boyfriend. I never liked that nigga. Always acting like he was the shit because he was some kind of broke ass dope boy wannabe. But a nigga that sold dope for twenty years wasn't no fucking dope boy to me. His old ass frowned up, crossing the yard with his eyes on fire and looking straight at me. . I didn't know what Tanya had told his ass, but he was mad, and I didn't give a fuck. I balled up my fists at my side, waiting for his punk ass to step wrong. Tanya was pulling at his shirt, but that didn't stop him from charging across the street. He must have known. "You fuck my girl, motherfucka?" he yelled the question and I didn't have but a few seconds before he was in the street, only Tanya in between him and me. "What the fuck are you talking about, Chauncey?" Serena was holding me back. Even though I did fuck Tanya I wasn't no fucking punk, and I didn't give a fuck if I had had his bitch in the bathroom calling my name; he wasn't about to step to me crazy. "Are you drunk, Chauncey?" Tanya asked, and the nigga had to be drunk if he thought I was gonna let him punk me. "Naw, I'm not fucking drunk. That nigga fucked Tanya, I already know it." He pushed her out of the way, trying to get to me. "How the fuck both of y'all disappear and then she show up smiling and shit?" I wanted to tell him it was because I gave her the dick that he couldn't. "Fuck you, nigga. You wanna fight over a bitch?" I said instead, but that was still too much, and his face changed like he was about to transform into a demon with horns pointed out of his head. If he hadn't been mad before, he was fucking fuming now, and so was Serena. "Wait, wait...So you did fuck her?" I shouldn't have said anything; now Serena had questions. "Naw, nigga, I..." Fuck... it was too late; he had Tanya out the way and was charging at me with his fists up. People came out the house as he got to me, swinging wild like some bitch. I ducked the first punch, but the second caught me in the jaw. Ringing in my head started, but I swung too, connecting two to his head and stepping back. Before I could throw another punch, somebody grabbed me and other family members held him back. "What the hell is going on out here?" Serena's mom said and tried to break us up. I broke free, grabbing my keys from my pocket. It was too many people here and I was all by myself. They weren't gonna jump me over this shit. "He fucked Tanya, upstairs in the fucking bathroom." Chauncey screamed as Serena's cousins held him back. Turning around, I saw it was Serena's step-father holding me. "Be easy, Son-in-Law. What's going on?" Her step-dad was a cool ass dude, but I knew he wasn't gonna be that damn cool after he found out what the hell was going on. Everybody was bundled up from the cold, but I felt hot as a damn volcano. "Landis...did you?" Serena's eyes were already filling with tears. "Naw, baby. I..." Everybody was talking and screaming at once, and then the worst question that could have been asked rang out of the crowd. "What the fuck is on his pants, then?" I looked down, and the white icing droplets on my jeans weren't food, but cum that had dried up and wouldn't come off even with me rinsing it off in the bathroom. Serena's eyes got big as basketballs, zeroing in on my jeans. It didn't help that the jeans were black and the white of the cum showed up like neon lights in the dark. "You bitch!" Serena went flying, charging at Tanya punching fast like a fan on high. Tanya didn't even have a chance to put her hands up before Serena was on her ass. Weave went flying and screams echoed through the block. With everybody distracted, I saw my way out; I had to leave before her ass turned on me. I ran to my car, jumping in and burning rubber off the block before anyone could realize what I was doing. The crowd of family in my rearview, with my girl fighting and rolling on the ground with her cousin, was the scene I ran away from, and it was all because of me. If only these hoes could leave me alone, I would be able to keep my dick in my pants. Glancing at my face in the mirror, I knew that probably would never happen. I was too fucking fine for that shit; bitches had been on me since my nuts dropped. And I didn't see that shit changing anytime soon.

Chapter 5

I drove through the city in a daze. Not sure whether to go home or just stay away for awhile. A text message came to my phone along with a million calls. I knew it was Serena with questions, and a ton of ways to curse me out. She knew I wasn't a one yard type of dog, but she'd respected it in the past. But I'd never fucked her family and she'd never had outright proof before. The text message said the same shit she always did when she was mad. "Get yo shit and get out of my house." She'd tried to put me out a million times already. I shrugged it off and kept driving. Circling the city, I formulated my plan of what I would say to her. "I didn't fuck her, she tried fucking me but I pushed her off." I tried out a few lies, but none of them made sense. All I needed to do was let a few hours zip by, and she would be calmed down and ready to talk. Dipping through some streets and taking the long way to my Mom's crib sucked up some time. Trying to figure shit out, I laughed at thinking of everything that had happened. Tanya's bitch ass boyfriend, Serena throwing hands, and me caught in the middle of the street with nutt on my pants. I just kept telling myself that the bullshit wouldn't make her put me out. One thing that all these chicks had in common was threats. She needed me at that house. All I needed was an explanation, to tell her I was sorry and I would put it all off on Tanya's hoe ass. Then she would forget about this shit in a week. Shit sounded great until she sent a picture. Like a nightmare, I saw my recording equipment outside in the snow. Shit had just gotten real. I pressed my foot down on the gas, racing to Serena's house. If this bitch fucked up my shit, I was gonna kill her.

Chapter 6

Serena was my kick-back, my money pot, and my fallback plan. She was supposed to be my get-right bitch for the tax season. I called her my girl, but that was only because she was at the top of the list now. Actually, she was just one of a few, but nobody had more drive and money than her. That's why she was in first position, and I had fucked that up. I raced to the house, thinking of all my hard work laying in the street. Now I would have an open spot on the roster for the winter. More pictures of my equipment in the snow only made me madder. I sped through stop signs and ran red lights, trying to get to her. These pictures of my equipment outside getting wet from the snow made my blood boil. All my hard work, all the money I'd spent on that equipment... all of it was bouncing around my head. I sped home and saw the police lights as soon as I turned onto the street. Serena's car was parked in the middle of the yard, and she looked like a fire-breathing dragon, throwing my shit on the lawn right in the snow. "What the fuck?" I screamed, running towards her until the cops pulled me back. She kept throwing shit: my speakers, mic, CDs, all laying in the yard like a garage sale. "Get all your shit out of my house. You fucked my cousin." The cops held me back, but I knew they wanted to laugh. "In my fucking momma's house, then you leave like a little bitch." Her momma and step-dad were there, too, on the porch and glaring at me like I was a monster. "Shit, she came on to me, man. I was in the bathroom minding my own fucking business." I struggled to get free as a basket of my clothes fell to the ground. "Oh, so you just slipped your dick in by mistake?" I heard somebody laugh behind me, but this shit wasn't funny. "So, ya'll gonna let her destroy my shit?" I asked the cops. "Sir, just get everything in your vehicle and please leave." One of the cops tried holding back his laugh. "Ma'am. Please go back inside until we come get you." "Fuck you, Landis. You'll never find another bitch like me." She screamed, ignoring the cops. Finally, her momma dragged her into the house and her step-daddy stayed outside for a second, watching me. Stan was a good dude, but if it was between me and his step-daughter, I didn't have shit coming. Wasn't shit I could say now. She was right, that I wouldn't find another bitch like her. Serena had three kids and always dropped three thousand dollars on me at tax time. That was the money I was gonna use to get my mix tape out in the streets. It was a little late for me to find somebody like that. I would have to start all over, and get it all solid by the end of January. "I need my damn house keys." Serena was back outside, screaming and trying to get to me. Her hair flying everywhere and she was cursing, but I was done with the bitch. "Here, and don't fucking call me when you need some dick either, bitch." Grabbing my shit, I tossed everything in my car. Praying shit wasn't too fucked up. Tax return time was right around the damn corner, and I was back at square one. It was time for me to find a new runner, and I needed to do it quick.

Chapter 7

My Momma's house was always where I could come back to. I'd never kept everything at one of these hoes' houses because their moods could change like the weather. But now all my equipment was stacked up with heaters and fans on it, trying to dry everything out. I'd called my nigga Dave to help me move shit, but all he did was laugh and ask questions, which was the last thing I wanted to hear right now. "So you fucked her...right there in ya girl's Mom's house?" Dave was my boy, but he had no problem calling me on my shit. But hearing him say it made things sound a lot worse than what it was. "Nigga,

I didn't mean to. It wasn't my plan." He said it like I'd meant to do this. "I was about to talk on the phone when her cousin slipped in." I laughed, giving Dave the info, but I was kind of sad about the shit. I'd put in too much time with Serena to give it up over some stupid shit like this. But me and her wasn't getting along, no way. Dave laughed, reminding me of some things he'd did that were way worse than what had happened to me today. We could probably fill a book with all the crazy shit that we did, but I was getting older. He was twenty-nine and I was twenty-seven. I wanted to get this money shit together. That's why getting my mixtape out there was so damn important. "Shit, man, why didn't you lock the damn door?" That was a good question. If I'd had the door locked than Tanya wouldn't have been able to come in on me. I couldn't worry about that shit now. What was done was done. Now I needed to find somebody new. "Man, I'm done with that shit, though. I gotta find somebody new." I picked up my phone, putting it on speaker. I needed to find a new victim, and the easiest way I could do that was through the chat line. "Voice

Mates. Please enter your mailbox code." The voice filled the basement, which wasn't that big. Just my bed, a TV, and now all my equipment with the washer and dryer in the corner. "Aww man, you still on that old shit?" Dave laughed extra hard now. Leaning over in the chair like he was about to fall out. "It's the season, man. I gotta get this mixtape going." I entered the code and hit a few buttons. "You gotta get online with it. Them bitch's on the chat line are tired." Dave was right. I checked the line about once a day, and it was the same hoes, the same message, and most of all, no money. "What, you got something else in mind?" Dave had a smile, shifting with his phone. "Hell, yeah, get you." He showed me some app on his phone. Had lines and lines of chicks. "It's a new one on here every day. They all work and got kids. Shit, I got three lined up ready to pay." That got my attention. Shifting around my semi-wet equipment had just made me realize how bad I needed this mixtape to work. Plus, by the looks of it, I might need some more recording equipment. I knew he had things he needed with his chick's money, and my mixtape was my main priority. It never failed that around this time of the year, shit always hit the fan, leaving us with no choice on how to get paid. Me and Dave were pretty much the same with our approach to women. Around this time we got down with one main chick, or a couple if they were talking right. We got in good with them, got they tax return money, and used that to do whatever we needed for the rest of the year. "Here, just go download it on your phone. It's a dozen of these apps." This shit blew my mind as I found what he was talking about and downloaded it to my phone. "So I can just get on an app and get a bird." We called the chicks that we got money from birds. They were so stupid they had brains the size of a bird's so we thought the name fit. Since high school, the name had lived on with almost every chick we messed with. Especially around this time, our motive was to get what we needed to keep surviving. But this would be the last year for me. After getting this mixtape going, I wouldn't need shit from nobody. "Landis McCall." My momma yelled my name from upstairs. She was supposed to be working today, and I hadn't expected to have to explain until tomorrow. Now it was back to this shit again, like some kid, while she yelled my name from the top of her lungs. "Yeah, here I come." I called up the steps. "I'm out, man. Hit me up tomorrow." Dave went out the basement door and I went upstairs. I hadn't told Momma I was moving back in yet. She'd probably saw my car outside still with the back seat full of some of my stuff. "Why is all that stuff in your car?" was the first thing she asked when I made it into the kitchen. "Well, hello to you too, Teresa McCall." She frowned at me as I gave her a kiss on the cheek. She hated when I called her by her whole name. "What I tell you about that?" I laughed as she put away groceries. My momma was a nurse and had been one since as long as I could remember. Twelve hour shifts, and sometimes she even worked out of town, so me being back home wasn't a big deal. I probably wouldn't even see her. "So, let me guess. You moving back in?" she asked. I never had to ask my momma to move back home. It was always understood that I would always have a key and whenever I felt like it, I could come back. "Yeah, just for a little bit." "Okay, cause you need to get yourself together anyway." She paused, staring at me. "Some little girl named Lovely stopped by here the other day. Hearing that name sent chills down my back. I hated that bitch, but she wouldn't leave me alone. "Aww, yeah. What she say?" I already knew, but I asked anyway. "She told me she was pregnant. Damn Belly was popping out of her shirt. Said it's yours." Momma's words stung me. I'd told that bitch to get an abortion but she didn't want to listen. "If that baby is yours, you gotta step up, Landis. You already got kids you don't take care of." Momma always had to bring that shit up. She put the groceries away while I sat and rummaged through the refrigerator, but I should have stayed my ass downstairs. "I told you they're not mine. I just need to get the test done." I'd explained this to her dozens of times. It was two chicks claiming to have kids by me, but I needed to make sure. I was gonna buy one of those kits out of the drug store, but I never had enough money. That was supposed to change when Serena gave me her tax money, but that wouldn't happen anymore. "You been saying that shit for years, Landis." Momma always shot it to me straight. I loved her, but she wasn't gonna spare my feelings. "My head hurts..."she stopped talking in mid-sentence. Her back was to me, but she swayed, her head dipping down. "Momma." I yelled to her, but she fell back. I caught her just in time before her head hit the floor. She was shaking, and I couldn't get her to talk. I could only pull my cell phone out of my pocket and call 911. "Please come. My momma, she..." I couldn't get the words out to the operator, as the only person that really loved me was passed out and might be dying.

Chapter 8

I was in the hospital, waiting to hear what was going on with my momma. Talking to her one second and calling 911 the next. I was in the room for what felt like hours before somebody came and talked to me. A doctor in a white coat with glasses that probably cost more than my momma's house. He said a bunch of words I didn't understand, until I heard 'bypass surgery' and 'heart attack' "Say what?" "We'll have to do the surgery soon. A few days from now at the most. She probably won't be back to 100 percent for at least three months. Some patients, it's sooner." The doctor said the words, but it took a while for my mind to digest them. I thought of her job, the bills, and who was going to take care of her? There was nobody else but me. I was the only child, and our family didn't fuck with us. Yeah, they all lived nearby, but the only time we spoke was when somebody was sick or dead. I was the only one she could depend on. "What brought this on?" I had to ask the doc. "Stress, poor eating, but she had stents put in a few years ago." My eyes lit up when he said that. "A few years ago." I ran through my memories, trying to remember anytime that Momma had been in the hospital, and I couldn't ever think of her being sick. "You didn't know?" I shook my head and he laughed. "That doesn't surprise me. Nurses are strong in that way. Probably didn't want to worry you." His words didn't make me feel better. This was all my fault. Them hoes coming past the house probably had her on edge, not to mention all the work she did. It was like she practically lived in scrubs and nurse clogs. "Can I see her?" I just wanted to look at her. See for myself what he was talking about. "Sure, follow me." I followed the white coat down through double doors and down the hall past patient rooms of people lying in beds and damn near in comas. Getting to Momma's room, I almost didn't recognize her. She never laid in bed during the day, and my mother had never been sick in her life. Coming in, I watched as she smiled at me, but it still didn't help. I was about to cry. The doctor shook my hand and left us alone. "Sorry I scared you, son." I had no words to say. If I spoke, I was going to cry. "It's gonna be okay. I'll be back up in no time." "Momma they said you have to have surgery. Some bypass or something." There was no way she was gonna be back up and running around. "They told you that. I told them not to tell you." She sat up in the bed, but started coughing. "Stay down. Chill out." She never listened. Always did too much and never wanted to listen to me. "I can't be laying down, Landis Jeremy McCall. Who is gonna pay the mortgage, the bills, and take care of my house?" "I will, Momma. I'm a man, I can do it." She laughed and coughed right in my face. "Son, you don't have a job. You have child support bills all over my living room table. Little bitches coming to my house left and right. How are you gonna take care of me?" Her voice cracked at the end, and I saw that the lady who was always so strong was now weak. Her laugh turned into crying. "I didn't raise you like this, Landis. I named you after your grandfather. A strong working responsible man." Her crying now shifted into yelling so loud that a nurse came in. "Is everything alright here?" she looked from Momma to me with a frown. We both said nothing, but she got the picture. "Sir, she needs rest, and can't be upset." I got the picture: she was throwing me out. "Momma, I'm gonna go home and get some of your stuff. But like I said. I'm gonna take care of you." I meant every word. "I hope so, Landis." She wiped her face with a tissue, but her voice said it all. She didn't believe me. I felt smaller than an ant, walking past that nurse glaring at me and leaving my momma behind. I left the hospital in a daze. Not sure what to do or where to go. I wanted to call somebody, but who the fuck was going to help me with my problem? Before what had happened earlier, Serena would have been here, right by my side, but I'd fucked that up. I didn't need her ass anyway; I needed some money. In the hospital parking lot, I sat in my car, stuck with nowhere to go. Getting a job wouldn't help me. Minimum wage wasn't going to take care of Momma, and that would take too long anyway. I needed money now. Thinking about my boy Dave and what he'd said earlier, I didn't have no choice. Going into my phone, I opened the app and started filling in the profile. It was time for me to get grimey. Every bitch that had money was gonna be a victim. I didn't give a fuck what I had to tell them, or how much dick I had to sling. I was going to get the money I needed, by any means necessary.

Chapter 9

FROM THE FRYING PAN TO THE FIRE

I was in the hospital with my phone ringing and vibrating like I was selling crack, but I was slinging something far more addictive. Dick was the number one drug of choice in the winter, and it was my job to capitalize on all the lonely bitches. The ratio of men to women was 16 to 1 or so, I heard on the news, and I could tell by looking around that it was true. Here I was on this new dating app for less than twenty-four hours, and my phone hadn't stopped ringing. I had to take notes to keep track of names and what I had told who. I felt like I was running a real business. Almost like I was trading stocks, but instead I was trading pussy and trying to cash in on my golden goose. In the hospital waiting room, I had a note pad, phone, and pens spread out on the table like some mastermind criminal. That's exactly how those people looked at me, too. They sat in their chairs judging me and whispering to their family about the black nigga with the ringing phone and headphones, but I didn't give a fuck about their rolled eyes or sideways glances; I had to get money for my Momma. She'd told me before she went in that her job would still pay her while she was out, and she had an insurance policy that paid out when she got sick. That was cool, but what about everything else? I still wanted to drop some money in her hand, and fill up the fridge with groceries without going and asking her for money. What the fuck do I look like as a grown man, asking my sick Momma for money right after a surgery? A damn fool, that's what I would look like. So I kept making my notes, looking at the clock and sending messages like this was a part of my job. I felt like a professional and I wasn't going to rest until payday. As far as the girls went, I hadn't met any. Everything had been done so far through the app or on the phone. I got pictures from all of them with more shots of pussy circulating through my phone than a Playboy magazine. I just needed to get Momma settled before I went out to scout some prospects. Plus, I was still narrowing down candidates from my specific list of qualifications. My criteria was pretty simple really: the chick just needed to have two or more kids, a job, and hopefully she wouldn't have no baby daddy drama in the way. Them niggas could always smell a check, and always became model fathers from December to March in hopes of getting a check. I never cared what the chick looked like. If she was ugly or fat, I could deal with that, just as long as she didn't stink and have roaches. I had to draw a line somewhere, but everything else was fair game. Momma in the hospital didn't leave me much time, but today would be the day I broke out. As soon as she got out of surgery, I was going on a journey for a bitch with a job and at least two kids. I needed a check like yesterday. Momma was in surgery, and I was in the waiting room lining shit up.

Chapter 10

Date was already in the works for tonight, and if things went right, this one might be taking the spot for Serena. Of course, Serena was calling like a bill collector to curse me out, but I didn't have time for the back and forth with her. What Momma had said to me a few nights ago had rocked my heart? She had never cried, and to hear her crying more because of things I did hurt me. She was right, that I was approaching thirty and I didn't have shit to show for it, but that was going to change. When this mixtape dropped, I was gonna be the man, I could feel it: I just needed a chance. I had two top hitters. One girl named

Lovely was number one, from her pictures and the stats she'd given me. Two kids, working two jobs, her own car and apartment, and her baby daddy was in jail for at least five years. Perfect. There would be no interference with what I needed to do. Plus, she was consistent on texting. While I was trying to make more notes, she called. "Hello." "Hey, boo." I was 'boo' already, another sign that this would be as easy as taking candy from a baby. "Whattup." I played it cool. This was her fourth time calling this morning, but you can't be too available to these hoes or they'll think you're desperate. "You gonna come see me tonight? My kids are gonna be at my Mom's." That sounded like a promising proposition. But I needed to make sure Momma was alright first. "Yeah, maybe, but I'm at work right now." This was something like work: I was here to see about my Momma and she was my job. "Aww, damn. That's what all that is in your background." She was thrown off by all the talking in the waiting room. "But shit, I really wanna see you." That's what they all said. We had sat up most of the night talking while I posted up in the waiting room on a cot in a corner. I was bored as fuck, but it kept me from worrying about Momma. "LA?" she called my nickname; I never told hoes my real name. "Yeah, my bad." "Did you hear what I said? I think we have a for real connection. I really want you to come fuck me tonight." That was like music to my ears. "Aww yeah, that's how you feel?" She was ready, I could tell. Who knew this shit would be this easy? "McCall family." A nurse interrupted my call. "Let me hit you back." Hanging up, I was at the receptionist's desk in seconds. There was no McCall family: I was it. My aunts knew about the surgery, but all they'd said was that they would show up some time today to check on her, but in the six hours of the surgery, no one had come. It was me, here by my Momma's side like always. The receptionist directed me back to the ICU, and going through those double doors and passing past people in comas made me want to cry. When I saw her, tubes coming from everywhere and her eyes closed, I thought I would pass out. This shit didn't seem real. "Mr. McCall?" A doctor appeared out of nowhere. "I know it looks a little alarming, but she is fine. Everything went exactly as planned. We will be taking the breathing tube out in the next day or so, but we just needed her to relax, so she is on heavy drugs to help her sleep." His words made sense, but what I saw didn't match what I was hearing. "We'll probably have her under for another twelve hours. But there are no issues right now. She's doing great," he reassured me. Stepping to the bed, I held her hand, wishing it was me in the bed. I didn't want her hurting, and she didn't deserve this. "Maybe you should go home, get some rest, and come back early so you're fresh when we get her up." It sounded like a good idea. My phone vibrating in my pocket told me I needed to go make some moves and get shit really rolling. "And you'll call me if anything changes?" "Of course." I nodded to his suggestion. He patted me on the shoulder and was gone, leaving me alone with her. "Momma, I love you. I'm here, okay." I told her, looking over all the wires and tubes. I wasn't really religious, but I prayed. Putting my head down and wrapping my hands around her limp hand in mine. "Please Lord, let everything I'm trying to do work and let my Momma survive this and be better than ever."

I wasn't sure if I was doing it right, but I needed what I was asking for to come true. If something happened to my Momma, I was gonna die. And if this mixtape didn't get out, I was going to be dead to. Two life or death situations, but one of them was definitely in my hands. Kissing my momma on the cheek and checking to make sure the nurses had the right number, and then I was gone. With my notes, phone, and determination, I was gonna fuck a bitch tonight, mentally and physically. Young LA was on the prowl, and that was never a good thing.

Chapter 11

She said her name was Lovely, but that was probably just a nickname. There was no way that a person would name their child that. That was cool, though, since I used my stage name, Yung LA, with all the random hoes I met. Her name could have been the Queen of England as long as she gave me this money. I ended up taking a shower and going back to the hospital to make sure Momma was alright, like the doctor had said. It was still early enough for me to do my dirt and still go back and check on my momma. Through the fresh snow we had, I made it to the projects where my first prospect lived. The only reason why I'd said I would come was because it was still daylight, and project chicks were always easier to deal with. Project chicks I talked to didn't expect much, and always fell for shit easier. She was at the door before I even knocked. "Hey." She appeared, stepping out onto the front porch, but I saw three dudes in the living room playing a game before she shut the door behind her. "Thought you lived alone?" I asked. "Yeah, I do. That's just my little brother and his boys. They come kick it over here sometimes." That was cool. I heard them laughing through the door. "So wassup with you?" she asked. Only if she knew the truth, but I kept it light. "Nothing much, just tired from working all day." She nodded at that. "You're cute. Just like your picture." That's what all the hoes said, so I was used to that. "You know most of the guys I meet look completely different." "Word, you look cute, too." I lied; she looked completely different today than in the picture she'd showed me earlier, but I was used to that shit. All the hoes sent the best picture they had with a good Photoshop to trap a nigga, but I wasn't worried about what was on her face, but what she had in her pockets.

"Come in. Too cold out here for all this talking." She was cool lookin at least; her face and body weren't completely fucked up, but I had dealt with worse. Her hair was in some type of curly black and blonde weave that hung down to her shoulders. I didn't like chicks with bad weaves personally, but this wasn't about what I liked. That and all the makeup and eye shadow caked on her face almost pushed me to turn around and walk out, but her juicy lips managed to keep me interested. Walking in the house, I saw the dudes were still on the couch playing the game and they didn't even bother to turn around and look my way. Looking around her house was cool: no kids around like she'd said, but toys were scattered everywhere so I knew she really did have some, and it was definitely more than one with all the action figures, teddy bears, and princess dolls piled in a corner. "C'mon, let's go to my room." I didn't object; the quicker I fucked her would make it the quicker I could wrap her around my finger. I walked behind her up the steps; her ass was fat and bouncy in some black leggings. I watched it jiggle as she walked in front of me up the stairs and to her room. "Sorry my brother is here." "No prob, that don't bother me." "Cool, take your coat off and relax." I did as she said and we started the usual bullshit that people do when they meet each other. I actually had to get to know her. What's my favorite color, where is my girl at, am I sure I don't have a girlfriend, am I a cheater, what am I looking for, and how many kids do I have, and a bunch of other questions. I lied about it all except my favorite color: it was green. She didn't need to know all that other shit, and as far as I was concerned, I didn't have any kids until I took these paternity tests, no matter what these hoes said. She told me she had three kids; baby daddy was a dead beat; her sister and her brother were all she had, and that she was looking for the right one. I wanted to laugh when she said that because I certainly wasn't the right anything for anybody right now, but I smiled instead, touching her on her knee as she laughed and touched my shoulder. Somehow, we graduated from touching to kissing and kissing led to her unzipping my pants. My dick never had a problem getting hard, and today was no exception. She played with my dick at first.

Teasing me like she was going to get on her knees and suck me up, but she didn't. Instead, she pulled my shoes, pants, and shirt off, but she still had on all of her clothes. Everything up until now was going good but now it seemed like she was one of those shy bitches. I hated when chicks talked so much shit over the phone, then changed it up when you were ready to get down. "Baby, you gonna take yours off, too? You shy or something?" I asked her and she cracked up laughing at that, so hard that she started coughing. I was about to ask her was she okay when she screamed. "Now!" She looked to the door at our right as it burst open. The same dudes we'd walked past downstairs bust in the room, guns out and pointed at me. "You better not move nigga or we are gonna blow yo shit off." I was frozen; I couldn't move a muscle if I wanted to. I was in the hood, at this bitch's house, and nobody knew I was here. I didn't have a gun, no money, nothing but a cell phone and a hard dick. Looking at her... the bitch was laughing like something was funny. This was my life on the line and she was laughing. I would have slapped the shit out of her if there wasn't a gun pointed at me. "Where is ya money at, nigga?" I had no words for they ass. I was about to die and nobody was gonna know where to find me. How I made the worst decisions all the time, I didn't know. But this was yet another one of my plans that was falling through. Just my fucking luck.

Chapter 12

"Man, I don't have shit, man." I pleaded with these niggas, especially with the tall one that pointed the gun at me. Literally, all I had were my car keys and my cell phone. There was nothing for them to take or steal, and if they took my car, it barely had gas in it. All the while, the other dudes searched my pockets with one looking in my coat and the other one looking through my jeans. My dick was now deflated like a popped balloon. "Damn, you really ain't got shit?" he pulled out my cell phone, which wasn't worth two pennies. The screen was cracked in a million places, and if it wasn't for my shitty fix of putting a screen protector over the glass, I probably wouldn't have been able to even use it. "Damn, bitch, you picked the brokest nigga on the chat line?" they looked at Lovely, whose arms were crossed, her face creased with a frown, but she didn't have shit to be mad about. Nobody was pointing a gun at her. "He told me he had a good job. Shit, I figured he had money." I wanted to jump up and drop kick this hoe, but I kept it cool. "Man, I got child support whipping my ass. I ain't got shit." I knew they could relate to child support, and my broke down cell phone showed that I didn't have a lot of money. "Just let him go, Tev, fuck it." Lovely, or whatever her name was, let out a sigh, giving me a pardon like I was some prisoner. "Aight, man. Get the fuck out of here. I don't wanna see yo ass over here ever again." He said that shit like I was actually going to want to be over here again. But I didn't say a word, pulling my jeans on and sliding in my shoes quicker than a bitch could snap their fingers. I was down the steps with my coat on and running to my car like somebody was chasing me. Burning rubber down the street and not bothering to stop at any lights until I was on the highway. I called Dave as soon as I could stop my hands from shaking. "Whaddup, boy? How is your Mom doing?" he answered, but that shit was secondary to what I had to tell him. "Nigga, I almost got robbed." I ran down the whole story of how I'd met her on the line and that she'd seemed cool. "That's what the fuck you get. You know better than to be in the projects fucking with them hoes. He was right; I had fucked up and broken all the rules. I was way smarter than that to go somewhere that I didn't even fuck around, just to get with a bitch. "You remember what house it was. You know we can go back up there." That was my boy Dave alright. He had my back one hundred percent, but I wasn't trying to fight or have no shoot out with them niggas. "Naw, I'm good, my dude. Just leave it be." I was out of breath like I had run a mile driving through the streets, but my line clicking stole my attention. "Hold up, D." "Yeah." I answered when I clicked over. "Landis." I looked at the phone again. It was definitely a number I didn't recognize. "Who is this?" "It's Beauty...I need your help." A chick off the chat line that had basically put me in the friend zone. "It's not a good time, B, I'm busy..." "I'll pay you. I just really need you to do something for me. I can't leave and do it because my kids are here." She was whispering and I knew that only meant her Baby Daddy was around, but being paid to do anything was music to my ears. "What is it?" "Come to my house and park, and call me when you get here. And hurry up, before he leaves." I wasn't sure what it was, but if she was paying, I was down. "Aight, I'm on my way." It was still light outside, but I felt like two days had went by. All this shit in one day was way too much. Sloshing around in the snow, I made my way to Beauty's house. As long as I was getting paid, this shit didn't matter. It was better than almost getting shot.

Chapter 13

I told Dave where I was going and he laughed. "I passed that bitch to you and told you to fuck her, and somehow you became her best friend." He laughed in my ear as I drove. I hung up on his ass because he was laughing so loud, but now as I pulled up, I felt like laughing at my damn self. In front of Beauty's house looked like a fucking nightmare. She was running out of her house after her baby daddy and they both were cursing each other out. He was slipping and sliding in the snow and she was chasing him, but the only difference was he had shoes and a coat on and she didn't "What the fuck do you want? Shit, a PlayStation ain't shit. I can buy you one, just stay." Beauty screamed, trying to keep this bum ass dude. I sat in my car behind my Momma's tinted windows, watching the whole scene. Her baby daddy didn't even look this way, and that was a good thing. In high school, he'd never liked me and always thought I was fucking Beauty, but we were just cool. Somehow, we seemed to get along, and out of all the females that I fucked, I never had that kind of relationship with her. It wasn't surprising since, unlike her name, Beauty wasn't all that pretty. She liked caking makeup on her face, thinking that would help her, but it only made shit worse. And she loved wearing fake eyelashes that looked like spider legs on her face. But one thing she had going for her was that fat ass, and that's what made that nigga give her three kids. "Bitch, are you crazy? I'm not fucking with you." That was him, punk ass Devon. He looked the same even though I hadn't seen him in a while, and like always, he was treating Beauty like dirt. In the doorway were her kids, crying and calling for her, but she didn't care. All she cared about was him, and I sat in my car watching the whole scene. I watched as the nigga pushed her down in the snow. He jumped in the car with some other dude I didn't know and drove away. Her face might have been fucked up, but Beauty was a nice person; she was cool and took care of her kids. She told me about all the stuff she did for his ass, and it never made sense to me why a cool chick like her could give her all to a no good ass dude like him. I got out of my car to help her up. She was covered in snow, no shoes, just socks that were brown from the dirt. "What the fuck are you doing out here like this, Beauty?" I was mad at her, pissed that she was out here falling in the snow with her kids still screaming and calling her name. "Can you follow him, please?" I looked at her like she was speaking another language. But the tears rolling down her face told me that she was dead serious. I'd saved her from catching fucking pneumonia out here, and she wanted me to run around following people. "Fuck, naw. Is that what you called me for?" I looked down the block to see the car sitting at the stop sign as if the dude was waiting on me to follow him. "Please...I'll pay you." She pulled out a stack of money from her pocket that was so thick that she could barely hold it. Some of the bills flew out of her hand and fell all over the sidewalk. I picked it up and tried to hand them to her, only for Beauty to push it back in my hand. "No, you keep it. Just go follow him...Tell me who he's fucking with." She pushed me. "Please follow him. I know he's fucking some bitch." I took the money. I was down to do anything for the cash. No matter how dumb the shit was. "Aight, I got you." She pushed me towards the car. "But don't get mad when you find some shit you don't like." Women always wanted to check phones, pockets, and follow a nigga, but they never liked the shit they saw. She wasn't listening. She was already running back to the house, and with the money in my hand, I was gone. Jumping back into the car and busting a U-turn right in the middle of the street, I went down an alley to a main street. I caught up to the car around the corner and down the next block. I stayed back a few cars, like some kind of detective trailing a suspect. Ringing my phone was Beauty, already wanting an update. "What's he doing now?" Beauty was on speakerphone, talking my head off. "I don't fucking know, he hasn't stopped yet." This chick was crazy and stupid, and I was just as dumb for doing this shit. "Hold up...I think they're stopping now." I told her as they slowed down. "Good; get pictures. I want to see this bitch he's fucking with." I rolled my eyes at the bullshit she was talking. Whether she knew who he was fucking with or not didn't mean she was going to stop fucking him. "Aight, whatever. I'll call you back then." I hung up on her, waiting to snap my pictures when his car came to a stop, forcing me to do the same. Parking a few cars back from them and on the opposite side of the street, waiting for something to happen, like some heart broken bitch. Who does this type of shit? But looking at the seven hundred and fifty dollars in the passenger seat brought back my reasoning. I sat back in the seat, Momma's tinted windows shielding me from anybody seeing who I was. I was thankful for that because her tired ass baby daddy didn't like me. I guess he thought I wanted to fuck her like everybody else. Yeah, she had a fat ass, but she wasn't my type, and more than anything, she was too broke for me. Every dollar she had went to him or them ugly ass eyelashes and blonde ass weave she wore down her back. Beauty and Devon were made for each other, and all I needed to do was get some pictures and get the fuck out of here. I thought maybe a bitch would come out of the house, but instead, they both got out of the car. It looked innocent, two dudes walking into a house, until I saw Devon grab for the other dude's hand. "What the fuck?" he pulled the dude close and hugged him. I took the pictures, but I couldn't believe what I was seeing. They kissed, grabbing at each other like a couple would do. All of this out in the open in broad daylight like he hadn't just been at Beauty's crib. I snapped away, zooming in on my broke down ass phone and hoping the pictures would be clear enough for her to see. Then Devon picked up some snow, throwing it at old boy. They ran, dodging the snow that the other one threw until somehow they ended up on the ground, rolling around and kissing each other. I snapped pictures like a photographer as this nigga rolled around on the ground with this dude like two fairies playing in a field. There was no way to explain this shit other than to admit that he was gay. I turned on the video to really get it all as Devon helped him up, pulling the dude into his arms with a kiss on the lips that was long and passionate, and I could tell there were some tongues rumbling around. Shit made me sick and happy all at the same time. Maybe this was enough ammunition for her to leave his ass, but I had seen enough. I drove past them as they walked into the house, not noticing me. I had to call Dave. "D, you'll never believe what I just saw." I ran it all down to him and he was laughing just as hard as I was. "Damn, man. I knew it was something wrong with his ass. And Beauty's ole dumb ass was gonna give him all that money." My ears perked up when I heard that. "What money?" "Her Grandma, man. Remember I told you her Grandma died and she got like ninety thousand?" I almost hit a pole when he said that. "Are you fucking serious? I knew she died, but I didn't know she was getting that much. How the fuck do you know that?" Dave only laughed and I knew what that meant. "You know she always had a crush on me and shit. I saw her in the store the other week and you know how that went." Dave would fuck anything. But what

Dave was saying made sense. "Man, she ain't fucking with me though, or I would be over there right now getting my cut off that pie." He was right. I pressed the pedal to the floor getting back to Beauty's house. "You still there, man?" D asked, but I was miles away, formulating a plan. I didn't even say bye to him; I just hung up. This was my ticket for the mixtape, help with Momma's bills, and anything else I needed: I just had to play it right. I parked in front of Beauty's house, looking over the pictures and putting my plan together. There was no way she was going back to this fun boy baby daddy, especially not with that ninety thousand in her pocket. At least not without giving me a cut.

Chapter 14

"Did you catch his ass?" Beauty was at the door when I got back. Still just as amped as she was when I left. I expected her kids to come running to the door, but there was no one behind her. "Where are the kids?" I asked, looking back behind her but seeing nothing. All I heard was some slow song playing and the smell of candles smacking my nose. "My sister has them for the night." "Sister?" I never knew she had a sister. All these years I only heard about her having brothers. "Yeah, on my Dad's side. We be off and on sometimes; that's why I don't talk about her, but fuck that," she waved off the sister talk. "Forget all that; did you see the bitch he is fucking with?" If only she knew the truth. "I saw a whole lot, but it's gonna take a few drinks to tell you about this." "Just what I was thinking. I got so much on my mind besides this shit. I was just about to open a bottle of Hennessey that I bought earlier." She bounced her fat ass all the way to the kitchen and I followed close behind. "We can drink while you show me what this bum ass hoe looks like." She laughed like she had already been drinking, which was a good idea. She didn't need to be sober when she got this news. "Let's get one drink in, though, before I lay this on you." This was only going to help my plan if she was tipsy. She did as I said, pouring us both a drink as she talked on and on about him and the argument. I didn't bring up the money she'd got. I knew Dave wasn't lying, and plus, I didn't need her figuring me out. "Aight, so show me," she said after swallowing the drink and slamming down the empty glass on the kitchen table. "Here." I passed her my beat-up phone and she started scrolling. I poured us both a drink as she started gasping. Standing up, she looked back and forth from me to the phone. "What the fuck is this, Landis?" she covered her mouth with one hand and held my phone with the other. "He's gay..." I wasn't sure if she was asking or telling me, so I said nothing. Waiting for her to connect the dots as the picture of them rolling around in the snow came up. "Wait a minute, maybe they are just play fighting?" I'd thought she would say something like that until I played the video for her. "If they're fighting, then why are they kissing?" Right at that moment, her baby daddy was lip-locked with another man. She looked at the phone and then set it down on the table. "How...how..." she asked softly at first, then raising her voice as the minutes passed. "I think I deserve a fucking explanation." She jumped up from her chair, running into the living room, but I caught her before she could get away. "But how couldn't he want this?" She stood, pulled away from me and twirling around. "This must be how I got it." I didn't understand that. What did she mean? She mumbled some other things that I didn't catch. I licked my lips readying myself for the show I was about to put on. On cue she started crying, her tears rolling down her makeup filled cheeks, creating an avalanche of brown makeup. She hugged me, crying in my chest so hard that all I could do was put my hands around her. "Beauty. I love you." The words came out easier than I'd thought they would. "You don't deserve to get treated like this." I pulled her away so I could look in her eyes. Hoes couldn't resist when I looked in their eyes and told them I loved them. "What do you mean you love me?" She stopped crying, rubbing her face and trying to understand me. This was my chance to steal the show. "I've always loved you, even back in high school; I just couldn't figure out a way to tell you." I lied, but I made it sound good. I could tell she believed me, the way her eyes shined, staring deep into my eyes. "Landis, I got so much going on right now. You can't love me...not if you knew the truth." I shushed her. "Let me treat you like a woman should be treated. I want to love you." I had her, I could feel it. Her body melted into me as I leaned forward, planting my lips on hers. We kissed like two lovers that had been apart for years, with Hennessey on our breaths and dirty thoughts running through my mind. I slipped my tongue into her mouth and pulled her closer. Palming her fat ass, she moaned as my dick was hard pressing in-between her thighs. Pulling her to the bedroom, we were tearing the clothes off each other, throwing them down as we went. She was naked in seconds in the bed, and so was I, with my dick poking out for the second time in one day. Except this time no niggas were gonna bust through the door and hold a gun to my head. She reached in her night stand handing me a condom and turning on her bedside lamp. "Put this on, and let me see you while you do it." I laughed but her hands on her hips staring at me without a glimmer of a smile showed she was serious. I did as I was told, sliding the condom on safe and secure. But like a drill sergeant she came over, getting to her knees and inspecting. "Damn girl you act like I got the plague." I laughed but she didn't. "Just gotta be careful these days." She must be drunk but we continued where we left off. Kissing and getting into the bed. I turned off the light so I wouldn't be distracted by her face. She didn't seem that bad without me looking directly at her, and with the

Hennessey swimming in my veins, it didn't matter anymore how ugly she was. I just wanted the money; that was all that mattered. "But this is going to change everything?" she whispered through the darkness. "How are we gonna be friends?" "Shhhh..." I slid on top of her. Feeling around for her wetness and parting her lips with my dick. "We're gonna be better than friends," I told her before I slid inside her. She screamed out, clawing at my back like they all did. Five pumps in and I was almost ready to cum. She had a snapper of a pussy making me thankful I suited up. I didn't need another potential baby momma running around. But hopefully this dick was enough to get her to come off the money. I felt like a prostitute, fucking for money but how much of a male hoe could I be if I was the only one that knew about it?

Chapter 15

The sun was back up and shining when I heard the phone ringing. I jumped, thinking it was my phone, but it was Beauty. Waking up to her arms wrapped around me scared the shit out of me and had my heart beating a hundred beats a minute, until I thought about what had happened. The pictures, the money, the Hennessey, and then the bed. "Hello?" she answered the phone, and I listened close to make sure it wasn't that nigga, but I could tell by the happiness in her voice that it wasn't him. "Naw, girl, you said you were gonna keep them until tonight." I turned over, drifting back off to sleep when I heard her name. "Lovely, you said you were gonna do it, I remember." I whipped back around, my eyes wide open. Maybe I was hearing things. "Aight, fuck it. Just bring them in. I'm here." She hung up, getting out of bed. Grabbing for her robe and tying it as my mind jumped in a million different directions. "Baby, what's going on?" I pretended to be concerned, but I needed to know who the fuck Lovely was and if it was the same person. "It's cool, babe, just my sister." SISTER...I screamed in my head. "Oh, you got a sister?" I pretended. "What's her name?" She laughed before she answered. "Lovely, if that makes sense. Remember I told you last night she was on my Dad's side. He likes those crazy names; I got a brother I never met named Messiah." She laughed, but I didn't see anything funny. "I want you to meet her." There was a knock at the door and Beauty was gone to answer it. Jumping out of the bed, my heart beat like a hammer in my chest. I had to get out of here. But it was only one way in and out of the house, no back door, and she was too high up for me to get out the window. I was fucking stuck. What was the fucking luck for me to find two sisters to fuck with? Out of the whole city, this shit had to happen to me. Especially a bitch that tried to rob me and kill me yesterday. I scrambled, getting my clothes on. "Think, Landis." I heard the voices coming closer. I jumped into the bathroom, hearing feet. Turning on the sink, I tried to buy myself some time until the knocks came. "Bae, I want you to meet my sister, Lovely." I changed my voice real quick, about to tell her a lie when my phone rang. "Bae, this is an important call. I'll meet her later." I was actually telling the truth this time. It was the hospital. "I gotta go to work, Beauty, I'll meet him another time." I heard the voice of the bitch who'd tried to kill me. Just like that, I was in the clear. I could breathe again, but not for long. "Hello." "Mr. McCall. "Yes. Is my momma okay?" my thoughts flipped flop back to Momma. I was supposed to be back at the hospital by now. "Yes, she's fine. I'm her nurse and she's asking for you." "I'll be right there." I told the nurse. "Well, she wants to talk to you." A little rustling on the phone and I hear my momma's voice. "Son, you there?" her voice was raspy but it was my Momma alright. "Yeah, Momma, I'm here." I sat on the side of the tub with my head in my hands. If I didn't have enough shit to worry about already. I was just glad she was talking. "I need you to go pay some bills for me and get the house set up. They said I can come home in in a few days." I couldn't believe that. She was coming home already. "Momma, you relax. I'm on my way up there and I'm gonna have everything ready." "Okay. I know you will. I love you." She sounded out of it, but hearing her say those words gave me the strength of ten men. I could do this, game this bitch, and get back at her sister for what the fuck she'd tried to do to me. "Love you, too, Momma." I hung up, coming out of the bathroom on a mission. "Baby, where you going?" I wasn't used to her calling me anything but Landis; this baby and bae shit would take some getting used to. "I gotta go to the hospital. My momma said they want some money to do a special treatment she needs. I'm gonna have to go donate some blood or something." I squeezed out a fake tear, sitting on the side of the bed and covering my head with my face. I didn't know where this shit was coming from, but it was working. "A new treatment. Doesn't she have insurance?" I said something, words that made no sense but whatever they were, it sounded believable enough to Beauty. "I don't have no money. How the fuck can I do this?" I asked her, my eyes filled with fake tears. She smiled, hugging me. "I got you." She left me on the bed and went to her dresser. Pulling out a wad of money and handing it to me. "Let me know if that isn't enough. I didn't tell you, but my Granny left me and the kids a bunch of money. I'm not gonna be broke no more." She smiled, crying now, too. I didn't count the money, but when I saw the hundred dollar bills, I shed some real tears. Standing up, I hugged her, kissed her, and hugged her tighter than a python to their prey. I felt like I'd won the lottery, and I had. I'd hit the Beauty number, the best number I had ever played.

Chapter 16

TRICKS ARE FOR KIDS

I heard somebody throwing up; the sound of chunks hitting the toilet woke me out of my sleep. Feeling around the bed, I felt that Beauty was gone – just sheets and pillows where she usually slept, but this was nothing new. We began every morning this way. She'd told me she had to wake up at six and take some damn diabetes medicine. She'd said it required her to be in the bathroom for an hour, with throwing up and some nasty ass diarrhea. Listening now to the toilet flushing, I knew why that gay ass baby daddy of hers didn't want to be here: it took a lot to deal with shit like this. But today I had bigger fish to fry. Today was the day I would record my mixtape. Beauty had given me enough money to go to a real studio and lay some tracks down. Yung LA was finally getting a shot, and for that I would stay with this bitch even if she threw up all over me and made me lick it up. So I still acted concerned about her ass. "You alright in there?" I asked her, rubbing my eyes. She cracked the door and yelled out, "Yeah, I'm okay," then slamming the door back again. If I didn't know better, I would have thought she was pregnant. But every time we fucked, she had me wrap it up. She'd even bought an extra-large box of condoms, saying she wanted us to keep using them, which was different for me. I didn't give a fuck how she wanted it as long as she kept dropping money on me. Usually, the chick I was with didn't want me to use a condom. I wanna feel all of you inside me. That shit got me in trouble every time, and was the reason I had paternity tests kicking my ass. It's something about having my bare dick in some juicy wet soft pussy that made my toes curl. Right now, looking at Beauty's ass made me want to go balls deep again, but the condom didn't do shit but get in the way. Maybe it was a good idea that I have a baby with this bitch. She had money and she'd told me there was even more coming, but I didn't want to deal with this being sick shit. It had been a week since I'd told her that her baby daddy was a fun boy, and now she damn near wanted me to move in, but this dick didn't come for free. I told her I needed help, my Momma needed money, and most of all, I needed this mixtape paid for. She came out, looking sick with her hair in a bonnet with bloodshot eyes. "So, are you supposed to be taking insulin shots or something?" She looked at me like she saw a ghost. "What do you know about diabetes?" Really, I didn't know shit about it, but my aunt had had diabetes and her legs were amputated. She'd had to take insulin and always check her sugar, but that was all that I knew. "Shit...really, I don't know anything; just asking, babe." "Well, talk about what you know. Cause I'm doing what I'm supposed to." She always got an attitude like that when I asked her about it. Watching her walk around the room, doubled over with her hand rubbing her stomach, was making me feel sick.

It wasn't my business and as long as she kept the money flowing, she could do whatever she wanted. I hopped up, ready to go take a shower and get gone. "Well, I'm 'bout to get up and head to the studio." She frowned up as I grabbed my clothes. "But you said you were going with me and my sister to lunch." Hearing about that bitch made my skin crawl. "I didn't say no shit like that. You know I got an appointment for the studio today." All this time, I'd managed to stay away so Lovely didn't see me again. I had something planned to get that bitch back for what she'd done to me, but I wanted to get this money first. "I know, but I was hoping you could come and eat, then go." She stuck her lip out like some sad baby, but that shit didn't work for me. "Aww, come on, baby." She slid to her knees in front of me, pulling down my boxers before I could protest. One thing I could say about Beauty was that she wasn't the best looking, but the bitch could suck a cheerio through a straw. Her hot wet mouth around my dick could have made me do anything but going to see her bitch of a sister that had almost tried to fucking kill me; that wasn't going to happen. "Naw, boo,

I can't." The slurp of her mouth filled the room until my cell phone started ringing. "I gotta get this...get up." I pulled her up, answering my phone. "Whatup, Dave." I hurried up and pulled my boxers up before she slipped my dick back in her jaws. It wasn't the time for me to meet her sister yet. "You still hitting the studio today?" Dave was like my hype man, on top of being my best friend. He saved the day just now, coming through and calling at just the right time. "Yep, man, I'm on my way right now." I pulled my clothes on, grabbing the money off the dresser and waving bye to Beauty. "I'll be back later." I winked at her and I was gone. Running down the steps, listening to Dave talk about the latest freak. "Man, she swallowed my dick and wanted to eat my ass but I didn't let her." I laughed at that shit. Starting the car and zooming away. "Yeah, I'm just now leaving Beauty's house and shit." He laughed at that, still giving me player of the year card for getting in with her ass. "Man, you are a fucking magician." Dave my boy told me as I drove to my Momma's house. "You got that bitch wrapped around your finger." It had been a week since I'd fucked Beauty and she was raining money on me like a fucking monsoon. "Man, it's too easy. You shouldn't have fucked up, or you would have been in my position." Dave laughed and I did, too. I was glad he'd fucked up with her so I could get a shot. "So wassup, now?" he asked as I made it home. "I gotta get Mom situated for the day and then I'm hitting the studio, man. I finally got some money to do this shit right." I could just see my mixtape being done. It was clear as day and I needed this shit completed ASAP. "A'ight, that's wassup. Tell Ma I said wassup." I pulled in the driveway and let Dave go.

Chapter 17

oing in the house, I found Momma was up playing some old school gospel. I'd thought she might still be laying down, but it seemed like as soon as she got home, she was dead-set on doing everything the doctors had told her not to. "Son, I underestimated you." Momma was home now and we were in the kitchen talking. I had taken care of everything, including her mortgage and all the house bills. If only she knew that it wasn't me, but Beauty and all the dick that I had been pushing on her that had did this. "I told you I would take care of you Momma." She smiled at that as I gave her more money. I wanted her to know I was for real about what I'd said, but the look on her face told me it was more to this. "Sit down, son." Shit, when Momma got serious like this, shit was never good. "What going on, Momma? I gotta get to the studio." "They found cancer." She blurted it out, not even giving me a chance to sit down. "It's treatable: I'm not going to die." "Damn, Momma, how long have you known?" She waved her hands like her having cancer wasn't important. "I've known for a little while, and they took it out while they did the bypass. I just didn't tell you." I put my head in my hand, trying to figure out what the hell was going on with my life. Just when I'd thought things were going great, I got news like this. "You should have told me, Momma." She looked better today than she had yesterday. Smiling and even getting herself dressed on her own. Every day, it was like she got stronger. "I had no time to tell you because you're always running the streets." I rolled my eyes at that bullshit. It was like she always said the same thing. "Momma, I'm not selling no drugs, I'm not robbing nobody." She laughed so hard she choked. "Oh, you think what you're doing isn't robbing nobody just because you didn't put a gun to the head?" I was confused. "Isn't that what robbing is?" She shook her head, her lip twisting like it always did when she got mad. "You see, the doctors told me that I need to keep my stress down." She took a sip of water, taking her time. "You are lying to these little girls. Telling them one thing and taking advantage. That's stealing, son." She stared straight through me. "Now, what if somebody did what you're doing to me?" I thought about it all, from the money, to the lies, and cheating. "But I wouldn't let nobody do that to you." I would put a motherfucka to sleep for doing that to my Momma. "See, every time you do that to them, you are doing it to me." Momma was talking crazy now. I got up, ready to leave. "Momma, you tripping. I gotta go." "Yeah, you're right. You do have to go...out of my house." She put a piece of paper in front of me. "Serena came by." She slide a sheet of paper to me. "She said she has a new number, but she also told me about what you did." I felt like punching a wall. I wanted these bitches to stay away from my Momma. Upsetting her and shit was what had put her in the hospital in the first fucking place. "Momma, I... "I don't want to hear it. I want you out of my house." I thought I didn't hear her right. "What did you say?" "I said I want you out of my house. You have one week to get your stuff together, but I'm done. I can't take this anymore." She pushed the money that I'd just given her towards the paper with Serena's number. "You're going to need that to get a place because you can't be wasting your life and staying under my roof." "So you gonna put me out over some bitch?" I was mad as fuck and I wasn't watching my tongue. "No, I'm putting you out because it's time for you to be a man." She stood up. "Because your father was the same fucking way, and I'm not going to sit back and let you piss your life away." She never talked about my Daddy. I'd found out from everybody else that he had more women than Macy's had dresses. "Maybe if somebody would have stepped in, he would still be here today." Her eyes started watering like they always did when she talked about him. "One week. Now get out of my face." She said it barely above a whisper. I didn't say shit in response, taking my money and the number, I slammed the door to the basement. I didn't need her, I didn't need this house, and I damn sure didn't need this raggedy ass basement. With a bitch like Beauty with more money than I could count, I didn't give a fuck about my Momma kicking me out. All I needed was to get the mixtape done, and I was going to be on. Long dick could change a bitch's attitude quicker than the weather, and I was gonna keep Beauty happy as long as I could, and then Momma would see I wasn't like my bum ass Daddy. I was better and smarter, because I wasn't just fucking hoes: I was getting money, too. "It ain't no comparison between me and that motherfucker." I screamed up the stairs, mad that she would even compare me to that motherfucker. I didn't give a fuck what she said. I was gonna get this mixtape and then I was gonna show her and everybody else.

Chapter 18

I'd dreamed of this moment. Being in the booth with the mic in front of me melted away all of my pains. My Momma was putting me out, I'd lost my main girl, and I was fucking a bitch I didn't want to be with, but none of that mattered after getting in that booth. The deep grey foam covering every wall looked like a masterpiece to me, and then there was the headphones covering my ears, playing the beats that I had listened to so many times. I'd waited so long to have enough money to get here, and now that I had the chance, I felt like the biggest man in the world. I spit the lines from my heart. Ones that I'd written when I was alone, hurt and begging for a way out. I was still pissed about what my Momma had said, but she didn't understand what it felt like, being a black man with no fucking options. I had no career, just passion to rap. Nobody would give me a chance and I wasn't the type to sell dope, so all I could do was use what I had. That's game, good looks, and a long dick. It sounded crazy, but I couldn't explain that to her, and the shit frustrated the hell out of me. So now, in the booth, I took it all out on the mic. I was on fire, breezing through songs with ease like a professional. I let all of my anger out on the tracks and made them explode. I could see through the booth into the engineer room as he and my boy Dave watched me. Nods of their heads and small smiles on their faces told me I was lighting shit up. If everything else in my life were as perfect as what I could deliver in the booth, I would have been in Heaven. "I think we got it. Wanna come out and listen?" the engineer asked me through the headphones. He was a ponytail, flip-flop wearing tattooed white boy, but he was a hell of an engineer. "Of course I wanna hear." I was back in the room with them, my songs bumping through the speakers as I heard line after line of my hard work. "Man, it's like I can feel every word," my engineer said, bobbing his head to the beat. That's all I wanted was somebody to feel what I was doing. If he could relate, then I knew somebody else could. That's all I needed was a chance. "Dave, how that sound, bruh?" I looked to my boy, but he was looking off into space. "You hear me, D?" I was waving my hands to bring him out of whatever trance he was in. "Yeah, man...that's tight." He looked at me with a blank stare, like his mind was a million miles away. I left it alone, looking back to the engineer and telling him what I needed. "I think a clean mix for the songs would be cool, and then maybe a chopped and screwed on the last one if you can." I told him, making me feel like a fucking boss. Calling shots and shit. The engineer gave me dap. He knew exactly what I meant. "Aww, yeah, man, no problem." I felt like we spoke the same language. Usually when I spoke to these hoes about rap or what I was trying to do, they didn't understand. I could stay in this space forever. "Cool, man, thanks a million times. I'll set up another session in a few days." I paid the man, peeling off fresh hundred dollar bills courtesy of Beauty. I had to get more money from her for the photo shoot and the mixtape cover, but my dream of a mixtape was so close I could fucking touch it. But my dog was in Lala land, not even paying attention. "C'mon, D. Let's go celebrate, dawg, on me." I hadn't been able to pay for nobody's drinks in a while, so I thought he would jump at that, but Dave was quiet. Walking out of the studio into the daylight, but everything felt dark as we walked to the cars. "You ever got a letter from the health department before?" Dave asked. "Health Department?" I didn't know what the hell Dave was getting at. "What you mean 'Health department'? Like for a job?" He took a deep breath, looking around as if someone was listening in on our conversation. "Naw, man. They said they need to speak to me. I called the chick back and left a message to see what she want." I shrugged it off. "Probably wanna tell you yo stank ass breath is hazardous, nigga." I thought that shit was hilarious, but Dave didn't laugh. "I'm serious, man. Like, I got a bad feeling." I didn't understand him, but his phone ringing interrupted any thoughts I had about the shit. I wasn't sure what bad feeling he could have, but I hadn't heard of nobody ever getting any letters from the health department. "You got it wit you?" Dave pulled out the paper so quick I thought he'd done a magic trick to make it appear. I read over it; only a few sentences, but it didn't explain anything, just gave a number for him to call. "My other patna said that it means somebody put me down on a list. Like they fucked me and they got a std." Hearing that almost made my knees buckle. "You burning or something, nigga?" I looked at him sideways, still laughing because this shit couldn't be too serious. He growled at me, pissed and snatching his letter back. "Man, quit fucking playing." He stuffed the letter back in his pocket. "I'm just fucking with you, man. I'm sure it's nothing'. If it was that big of a deal, they would have called you. They probably send this shit out like stores send out coupons." He nodded at me, his frown disappearing a little bit until his phone rang again. He answered it so quick it didn't even get through a full ring before he was talking. "Hello....Yes, this is him...Okay, I can come now...but can you tell me what this is about?" Dave asked whoever he was talking to, but I could tell by the look on his face that it wasn't much news. "Okay...thanks." He hung up, sifting his keys out of his pocket like a mad man. "I gotta go, dude. I'll catch you later." "What did they say?" He shook his head. "Nothing; just that they'll explain when I get there." "You want me to roll wit you?" He shook his head no, ducking into his car and speeding off. Dave was hella dramatic like that. He always overreacted to the pettiest shit, so it was cool that he didn't want me to go because I could celebrate in my own way. I called Beauty as I got into my car. I might as well go out with the chick that was responsible for all of this. But when she answered the phone, she sounded worse than Dave. I could tell she was crying. "What the fuck is wrong with you, Beauty?" "Everything; it's just all fucked up." Why on the day when I was trying to be happy after everything that had happened with my Momma this morning did every motherfucka around me have to be in they feelings? "Man, like what...?" I was ready to hear some long ass sob story as I drove. "It's such a long story, Landis...I mean, it is so crazy." She cried, blowing her nose and choking. "I'm on my way there, man." "Okay, you know I love you right?" I looked at the phone, wondering what the fuck was up with this bitch. I told her I loved her, but I didn't for real, and hearing her say it made my stomach hurt. "Yeah...and I love you, too..." I switched lanes through traffic, lying to her ass. "Okay, that's all that matters." Fuck, everybody acted like they were gonna die and were killing my damn mood. "A'ight, man, I'll be there in a few." I let her go, hanging up before she could respond. These motherfuckers were killing my vibe, and the next time I rolled to the studio, I wasn't asking nobody to come and I wasn't inviting no damn body. My phone rang again, Serena's name scrolling across the screen. Since I'd left my Momma's house earlier, she had been blowing my cell up, but I hit ignore on that bitch every time. The letter she'd left at the house was in the glove compartment and I had no intentions of reading it. I was done with the bullshit. As soon as I got the mixtape done, I was gonna fuck with Beauty for just a little while longer, and then I was out. A nigga like me didn't need to be tied down anyway. I'm a star and it's time I start acting like it.

Chapter 19

"My B.D. is in the hospital," she blurted out as soon as I walked into the house. I wanted to tell her I didn't give a fuck, but I pretended to care. "Aww, yeah? For what?" She looked at me crazy, as if I should know. "Just some things." I didn't give a fuck if that nigga died for all I cared. I just wanted to keep my spot on her team. I walked over to her, looking down with my chest poked out, trying to look jealous. "So what...you gonna go see him or something?" She sucked her teeth. "Naw, I'm just saying. I gotta tell the kids when they get home." Her little crumb snatchers were always gone with her Momma or somebody else. It was almost like she didn't have kids, which was cool with me. I wasn't trying to be nobody's Daddy, especially when I might have kids of my own running around. My next order of business was to get those paternity tests done, but that shit would come after I got my mixtape done. Beauty was acting strange, looking off out the window with the same fucked up look that Dave had had. "Then why you looking all paranoid and shit?" I asked her, but she waved me off. I pulled her close. "You know you my girl, right?" I said that shit because it sounded good. Made it seem believable that I really wanted to fuck with her. "Yeah...I know that." She smiled up at me. "You love me, right?" I pulled her close. "Yeah, of course I do." "Then I could tell you anything and you would stay with me." I didn't flinch, looking straight in her eyes. "Anything, boo. Just tell me." "You say that now...but what I have to tell you is pretty rough." Her phone rang just as she said it, and so did mine. "Let me get this." She pushed back from me and I grabbed my own phone as she answered hers. Whatever she had to tell me, it didn't matter as long as she funded the mixtape. Looking at my phone, I saw the number didn't look familiar but I answered anyway. "Who is this?" I hated new numbers, and always figured it was a bitch playing on my phone. "Landis....it's me." I searched my memory for who the fuck this "me" could be. I knew a dozen hoes that thought I specifically knew them. "Who?" as I said it, Beauty looked at me with furrowed eyebrows. One thing about that bitch was that she was nosy, but they all are. She was talking to one of her friends, so I stepped out of the room. But my caller was getting an attitude. "So you don't even know who this is?" "I'm kind of busy, so come on with all the games." I shot an attitude right back. "How the fuck do you call me wanting me to play the guessing game?" She took a deep breath. "It's Serena, fool." I smiled at that; Bitch couldn't stay away. I knew she would figure out a way to get through to me somehow. If nothing else, Serena hated being ignored. "You told me to never call or come by your spot again. That meant you were dead to me, so naw, I don't know what you sound like." I lied. I had her voice etched in my brain. She laughed at that. "After three years, you don't know what I sound like." She kept laughing like I was a fucking comedian. "So you the one with the attitude when you cheated on me? Now that is hilarious." "Whatever, man, is that what you called me to say? 'Cause I'm busy." "Landis, I'm pregnant." I looked around to see Beauty on the phone. What she'd said was so crazy I felt like the whole world heard it. I had to make sure I heard her right. "You're what?" "I just found out today. I'm pregnant with your baby." I felt like my feet were stuck to the floor, but Beauty's laughing brought me back to life. I couldn't let her find this shit out: it might mean that she would stop funding me. I snuck outside, still holding the phone. "Landis, you still there?" "Yeah... like...how far along are you?" Out of all the chicks that I was with, I just knew this baby was mine. I could feel it. "Six weeks." I counted in my head how much that would cost. I knew the rules at the clinic like the back of my hand. An abortion with two months or less of pregnancy would cost me $425. I was in that abortion clinic so much it was like I worked there. "I just wanted to let you know. 'Cause I know what happened wit you and Tanya wasn't your fault." I couldn't believe she was saying this shit. I looked around in the cold night, waiting for some cameras to pop out and scream surprise. This had to be a joke; no way that she was trying to give me a pass. "I was trying to tell you that. It was just a fucked up situation." "You didn't have to fuck her..." "That's old shit, Serena. Either we gonna talk about here and now, or I gotta go." I looked through the window to see if Beauty was still on the phone and she was. Chatting away and laughing like a rich bitch with no cares in the world. "I just want you back. I don't want to raise this baby on my own." Raise the baby...who said anything about having it? But I played it cool. "I got a lot going on right now, Serena. I don't know if I would be a good Daddy. Shit, I don't even have a job." I lied; my job was fucking the shit out of Beauty, and I was getting paid very well for it. "Don't say that. You could be the best Dad." She'd always had faith in me like that. Always trying to push me. For real, she was the one that bought most of my studio equipment and had helped me buy a couple of beats for the mixtape. Serena was really the only chick that believed in me, and if she didn't already have kids, she probably would have paid for the mixtape already. But my phone beeping took my attention. It was Dave, probably telling me that everything was cool and he wanted to go out. "Hold on a sec, Serena." I clicked over to see what my boy Dave wanted. "Hello." "Nigga, where you at?" Dave was screaming like he was in pain. "I'm at Beauty's house, man. Wassup?" I was ready to fight, hearing my boy sound like that. Not sure if somebody was fucking with him or if somebody had died. "You at that bitch's house.... I'm on my way." Before I could say okay, he hung up. I clicked back over with Serena. "I'm back; my bad." "Landis, just come home." She was crying, and I could picture her on her knees begging for me to come back. Looking through the window at Beauty, I knew if I stayed, she would pay for my mixtape. But I couldn't say I didn't miss Serena. We had a bond and she knew me better than any of these hoes. "We gotta talk about it." Despite anything, I needed to be nice to her. If I acted like an asshole, she might not have the abortion and then I would really be fucked. "Okay, when can you come over...Tonight, maybe?" "Yeah, I'll see what I can do." I heard the screeching tires of Dave's car before I saw it. A few seconds later, he was racing on the street like a racecar driver. He stopped in front of the house, hopping the curb like somebody was chasing him. "Let me hit you back." I hung up on Serena, walking down the steps to see what was up with Dave. He looked like a fucking fireball, all red with his face frowned up. "Where that bitch at?" He asked, jumping out of the car. "Who, bruh?" "Beauty, nigga...Where is she at?" He didn't wait for me to answer. Pushing past me, he leaped up her front steps and was in the house. I had to run just to catch up to him, but when I got inside, it was already too late. "You bitch!" he screamed at her, jumping into the living room and grabbing her in a chokehold. "What the fuck, Dave, let her go!" I grabbed him, pulling him off as Beauty fell to the floor. Dave was screaming so loud it was like he had a megaphone attached to his mouth. "So you wasn't gonna tell me, bitch? You let me do that shit and you didn't tell me?" She said nothing, scrambling to her feet as I tried holding Dave back. "What the fuck you talking about, Dave?" "That bitch gave me AIDS!" He screamed it, lunging back towards her. But I had to be hearing things. "What...AIDS?" I couldn't piece the shit together. He pushed me back, freeing from my hold. "That's what the fuck they wanted at the Health Department. The bitch put down a list of motherfuckers she had been with and I was one of 'em. They fucking tested me right there... right fucking there, bitch." He pulled out a letter, handing it to me. I skimmed over it, reading down to a list of shit, but when I saw HIV with a positive next to it, my eyes went blurry. "Yeah bitch. I got the damn test results back on the fucking spot." Dave screamed at her. "I'm sorry...I'm so sorry." Beauty was crying, covering her mouth with her back against the wall. "Awww, you sorry, bitch. I'm sorry, too." Dave pulled up his shirt and pulled out his pistol. I went mute when I saw the gun. The shine of the pistol almost blinded me. He pointed it and everything I could try to say left my head. "Bitch, you wanna kill niggas, huh? You didn't tell me you had that shit." "Please...I'm sorry." Tears were falling down Beauty's face like rivers as she begged him for her life.

"Bruh..." I found my voice. "Did you fuck this bitch, Lan?" I didn't know what to say. I'd already told him I fucked her; I used a rubber every time, but that didn't mean shit. I felt sick, like my stomach was gonna jump out of my throat. "Did you fuck her?" he yelled, still pointing the pistol at Beauty. "Yeah, man..." "Then you got that shit, too. She gave it to both of us and didn't say shit." He looked back at her, fire in his eyes. "She killed us nigga. We as good as dead." I thought back on all the mornings and all the pills. She'd never tested no damn blood sugar, and I didn't see no insulin needles like my aunt had always had. It wasn't no damn diabetes she had; it was AIDS and she was fucking hiding it from me. The gay baby daddy and the box of condoms all swirled around me. My head was pounding, hearing his words, but I tried to talk to my boy. "Dave, man...calm down, my dude, you don't wanna do this." "Yes, I do. I wanna kill this bitch like she trying to kill me." "Please please...." Beauty said over and over, crying and begging for Dave not to do something he couldn't take back. Her eyes were red from crying, her voice hoarse from pleading with him. But I knew Dave too well; if he pulled out a gun, he had every intention of using it. I had to talk him down before he murdered her. "I'm dead...I'm a motherfucking dead man." He walked around the room, waving the gun and talking to himself. I didn't know what to say to him to calm him down. Beauty tried moving, but Dave was on it, crossing the room and putting the gun back in her face. "You gonna run, bitch, I'll shoot your mutherfucking head off." "But Dave, man. Please, bruh...we can fix it." I tried talking to him and calming him down. "Ain't no fixing this shit, man. AIN'T NO FUCKING CURE!" I heard the words: everybody knew that there was no cure for what we called the "Monster" in the hood. "I know, bruh, but..." "But shit...I'm dead... it's over. I might as well end it now." He clutched the gun so tight that I could see every muscle in his hand tighten. Beauty's phone rang and it sounded like the bells of heaven; it was like a sign from God. For a moment, he looked away, and it was my chance. I grabbed the gun, trying to wrestle it from his hands, and Beauty screamed behind us. My back hit the wall, holding the gun as Beauty tried to move out of the way when he suddenly pulled the gun from me. I tried to jump in front of Beauty, and push her out of the way, when I heard the pop. Beauty screamed, a deafening high pitched yell that shot through my body. "Bitch, you made me shoot my boy. Lan...Lan..." I didn't even notice I was shot until I looked down. The blood soaking my shirt. Beauty grabbed me as I fell to the floor, the pain shooting down my right side. I looked at him, wanting to speak, but my mouth couldn't move. "I killed him, shit... shit..." he screamed, lifting the gun. "You made me kill my brother." I heard him say as my eyelids lowered. I felt so tired, I just wanted to close my eyes for a minute, but I found a way to keep them open. Only a slit of light got through my half closed eyes as I felt Beauty holding me and crying. I saw the gun, the glint of the handle again, as Dave held it up. "Please...no..." Beauty begged, but it was too late. "You made me kill him...I'm dead...we all dead." He lifted the handle and there was another pop of the gun. Blood splattered over us like a shower and hit the wall. The loud thud of a body hitting the floor was that last thing I heard before it all faded to black.

Chapter 20

GRACE AND MERCY

I had to be dreaming. All around me was fire, but somehow we were at Beauty's house, but it was covered all in fire. I kept asking him why was the house on fire. Why were we burning? But he didn't answer. The scene kept playing over in slow motion like a dream. I kept seeing Dave, face red, gun shining in his hand, but this time we didn't fight. Just the flames were around us as he apologized. "I'm sorry I shot you." He kept saying. Beauty wasn't there: just me and him. "It's cool, let's just go." I tried to leave, but my feet wouldn't move. "I can't, Lan. I'm already gone." Gone? I didn't understand what he meant as the flames got higher around us. I fanned off some flames, trying to get my legs to move. "Naw, dang. You're right here." I tried talking to him, but he faded away, gone like a cloud of smoke, and the room disappeared. My eyes would flutter open and I saw doctors, police, people talking, but I couldn't move or say anything. I was in and out until finally somebody called my name. "Landis, can you hear me?" I didn't know who the voice belonged to. I moved my mouth, talking slowly, barely at a whisper. "Yes." "Do you know where you are?" I felt pain; my eyes opened fully and I focused on the light. Everywhere around me was light and this intense beeping. "No..." my mouth felt dry like a desert. "You're in a hospital. You have been shot." That's when it all came flooding back. Dave trying to shoot Beauty, us fighting over the gun, then the pain, the screaming, and then... "Dave." I called his name, looking around the room and hoping he was there to tell me the shit had just went bad and he didn't mean it. The nurse was towering over me, her face confused. "Dave... Dave..." I needed to see my boy. Tell him I wasn't mad about what had happened. "Let me go get your family." The nurse left me in the room of machines. Looking down, I saw my clothes were gone, a gown and white sheets was in their place. Then the pain; my head and my neck were pounding. I had to get out of here. I tried moving, but the pain shot up the side of my arm, making me scream. Rushing in was the nurse, with my Momma right behind and a face I didn't expect. Serena was there, her makeup running streaks of tears down her face. "Mr. McCall. Please don't get up yet." I pulled back the sheets anyway. I needed to see my legs. "Am I paralyzed? What the fuck is going on? Where is Dave? Momma, where is Dave?" I remembered hearing another shot, feeling the thud of something hitting the floor and Beauty's screams. "No, you're not paralyzed...just. Let me get the doctor. Please, don't let him get up." Tubes in my arm as I reached out for my Momma. "Baby, calm down." Momma came to me, hugging me and pulling me into her arms. Serena was so close; I touched her, giving her a hug too with my free hand. "I thought...baby, I thought you were..." Momma broke down, but nobody was answering my question. "Where is Dave?" They both looked at each other. "Is he hurt? I know they probably locked him up, but he didn't mean it." "Baby..." "Momma, he didn't meant it. Tell the cops to come in here. I can explain it all." "Baby..." Momma shook her head. "David is...." I pulled myself up, trying to lift my feet out of the bed. She was taking too long. "Just go get 'em, Momma, and I'll explain it all. That bitch, Beauty. It's all her fault." I felt sick even thinking about her. My face went hot, remembering what Dave had said she did. Momma rubbed my head. "David didn't make it, baby." "Make what?" I didn't understand. Dave could do whatever and be whatever. He was my right and left hand. My best friend since I could remember. What didn't he make? "He lost too much blood; it was nothing they could do." I searched my Momma's face. Saw the tears. Looking back and forth between her and Serena, I remembered that last shot and the thud on the floor. "No...NO...NO!" He couldn't have. Not my boy, not Dave. I pushed my Momma away, lifting myself up out of the bed. My bare feet on the cold hospital floor. "Son, you gotta rest; you just had surgery." Momma begged me, but it was too late. I was on my feet. "I gotta go get Dave. Y'all tripping." I stood up. My legs shaky, and my head pounding and dizzy. "He's dead, son...he's gone." I didn't believe her. "NO; don't say that!" I screamed. "He didn't mean it." The nurse and the doctor came in as I was yelling, and they were trying to get me back in bed, but I wasn't doing shit until I saw Dave. My best friend wasn't dead. "Mr. McCall, you have to calm down." "No, get Dave." I pushed past them all. Making it to the hallway stumbling and falling. "Dave...DAVE..." I screamed his name. I wiped away the tears in my eyes. I knew D would be coming around a corner, smiling and joking like always. But all I saw was three nurses running towards me. One with a needle, bum rushing me like I was a crazy man. "No... no...DAVE, MAN, WHERE YOU AT?!" I screamed, my eyes blurry from the tears. I felt the needle and saw Momma and Serena crying and begging for me to calm down. This couldn't be real. My best friend, my brother, they were telling me he was gone. My eyes dimmed again, and my body went numb as I tried to fight, but it was useless. With everyone standing around me, I faded to black.

Chapter 21

I woke up with Serena at the side of the bed, her head down and asleep, her holding my hand with a Bible laying on my bed. She was the last person I'd expected to see. After what I'd done to her, she should have been the one who shot me. What Beauty did, Serena would have never done to me, but I was chasing some money. I rubbed her head and she opened her eyes. "You›re awake," she smiled at me, squeezing my hand. "I'll go get the doctor." She started to move, but I grabbed her hand. "Tell me what happened. What did they say?" If Dave was really gone, she would tell me the truth. The girl, or whoever she is, said that Dave came over hysterical about something, and was trying to shoot her and you saved her." I remembered that part. I needed the rest of the story. "No, the other part." She swallowed hard, wiping her face. "He shot himself at the scene and...they pronounced him dead." Her eyes watered a bit. "Now don't go crazy again, okay? I can't take seeing that." She squeezed my hand, standing up. "Can you tell me what happened?" she asked. I looked in her eyes, wondering why she'd even bothered come here. Why after all the shit I did was she so in love with me? I wasn't sure, but I was done lying. "The chick...Beauty." I felt sick saying her name. "Dave said she gave him HIV." Serena gasped, covering her mouth. "Old girl you went to school with?" I'd forgotten that Serena knew her. I nodded, trying to find the words to continue as I replayed what I could remember. "He pulled out a gun. Mad ready to kill her. I don't give a fuck about her, but I couldn't let my boy get a murder charge." I remembered the look in Dave's eyes. How crazy he was, and seeing the stats on the paper would have probably made me the same way. "So when I had a chance, I tried to grab the gun from him. We wrestled with it and it went off, hitting me I guess." I remembered the feeling as I touched my head. It was shaved down to the skin, as I felt bandages on my head and down to my neck. "Don't touch it. Doctor said you will recover just fine." I didn't even care about my head. My other issue was what Dave was talking about. Did I have HIV? I'd wrapped up with Beauty but that didn't mean shit. I shouldn't have fucked with her, I actually shouldn't have fucked with half the bitches I'd messed with. "Where's my Momma?" I knew she was probably losing her mind by now. "I told her to go home and get some rest. She's still not 100 % from her surgery. Why didn't you tell me she was sick?" I didn't tell Serena because she'd put me out, we weren't together, and it was right after I'd fucked with her cousin. "We were...you know." She nodded, understanding what I meant as I examined the IV in my hand. "The bullet lodged in your head. They took it out and there was no damage. You're gonna be okay." I nodded at that. Shit felt awkward, and for some reason I wanted to apologize for every fucked up thing I'd done to her. Out of all the hoes I'd fucked with, Serena was the only one here. Nobody else cared about me, and I realized that shit now. "Look, it was even on the news." Serena turned up the television showing Beauty's house. Ambulances and police cars all around, blocking the house off with yellow tape. "A love quarrel turns into one man dead and another one injured." It wasn't a lover's quarrel; it was a fucking confrontation of a bitch that was around spreading AIDS around like candy. "Turn that shit off." I told Serena, and she did. "That damn bitch." "Who?" "Beauty...she killed my boy." Serena shook her head, looking at me like she wanted to say something. "What?" "How is this her fault?" I felt my face get scorching hot. "If she wouldn't have given Dave that shit, he would still be here; I wouldn't be shot." I raised my voice and Serena stood up. "I'm not defending her, but can't nobody just give you AIDS. Dave fucked her, probably without a condom, 'cause that's what y'all dumbass niggas do." She shook her head, walking over to the window. "It could have been you, all the bitches you fucked. Hell, you even gave me a disease once." I remembered that shit like it was yesterday. Serena calling me crying, saying she had chlamydia and that I gave it to her. Fucked up part was I didn't know where I got it from. I rubbed my head, feeling a headache coming on. "You bringing up old shit, man. I'm talking about my dead best friend." She spun around quick like a human tornado. "I'm talking about you. You could be dead, you could be the one with HIV, shit, you might have it and we don't know. I'm talking about you fucking my cousin in my Momma's house, I'm talking about this baby in my stomach. Motherfucka, I'm talking about the decisions you make." She screamed at me, her voice so loud that I knew the nurses heard her. I couldn't argue with that. I had fucked up too many times over the years and I couldn't defend that. "So what the fuck do you want me to do?" I asked her. She grabbed her purse, and slid on her coat. For the first time, I saw a small bump on her belly. She really was pregnant. "Landis, I just want you to grow the fuck up." She stared at me as if she wanted to hit me. "Dave's funeral is in two days. Maybe seeing your friend in a casket will show you this shit isn't a game." With that, she left, leaving me alone with the small hum of the television and my feelings. I wished that the nurses would come in and give me another shot. Being knocked out was better than dealing with reality. I was shot, my friend was dead, and I might have HIV. I couldn't see how shit could get any worse.

Chapter 22

"Mr McCall?" I woke up in a sweat to a man in a black suit. "Yeah." "I'm Detective Bryant. I need to ask you a few questions." I'd figured they would show up sooner or later. If he had questions, I had a few of my own, like where the fuck was that bitch Beauty and what were they gonna do with her. I pressed a few buttons to lift me up in the bed. "Yeah, ask away 'cause I got some questions, too." "Can you tell me how the night of the incident began?" I thought back, now putting pieces together on shit that I didn't even think about before. On how sick Beauty was, how she'd told me it was diabetes but that had never made sense. I could have checked the medicine bottles, but I never gave the shit a second thought. All I wanted was the money, and now I had more problems that money couldn't fix. I told the detective how I'd gone over to Beauty's house and how shit had progressed from there. "Now, when you tussled for the gun. Did it seem like he tried to shoot you?" "No, he wasn't' trying to shoot me. He wanted to shoot her, but...I tried to stop it." I still didn't know why I'd done it. He could have killed that bitch and I wouldn't have cried. "She told me she had diabetes and that's why she took medicine." He wrote my words down with his pen scratching furiously across the pad of paper. "So Ms. Jackson didn't tell you she was HIV positive?" I shook my head, thinking back to the big box of condoms. "We always had protected sex, but she never told me, and Dave said she never told him. Until...." the paper from the health department was etched in my brain. HIV stood out on that paper like it was highlighted in neon. "So you believe that she infected Mr.Eads on purpose." I shrugged at that. Who knew what that bitch was trying to do? "I don't know if it was on purpose, but he said he got it from her. The health department told him so." The officer kept writing. "Where is she now?" It wasn't like I wanted to see the bitch. I was just curious if they had her in handcuffs yet. "She was just released from the hospital for shock and hysteria." The bitch should have been hysterical. "So what happens now?" I was ready to hear about that bitch going to jail, being charged with murder or something. "Well, that's all really. We will investigate, but it's pretty much a cut and dry case." He talked like he was confused, putting his notepad back in his pocket. "So you're not going to arrest her for not telling motherfuckas she got HIV?" He shook his head. "We will investigate, but honestly, Mr. McCall, it's unlikely that we will. Are you positive, sir?" That was a question I didn't have the answer to. "I'm not sure yet. But I'll find out." "Well, here is my card. We are going to investigate and you let me know when you find out." I took his card, but I already knew what was going to happen. The bitch was going to get off for doing this to my friend. "Word of advice, man..." the detective said. "You gotta find one good girl and hold on to her for dear life. I see this shit happen more often than you would think." With that he was gone, and it made me think more about what Serena had said. This was all my fault for putting myself in danger. I had to face that: Serena was right.

Chapter 23

I had been to a dozen funerals, but this one was different than the rest. Fresh from the hospital, I walked in to pay my last respects to my best friend. It wasn't real till I saw the casket; as we filed in, people were already crying. I kept thinking that maybe he would come back one day with a smile and saying some crazy shit like he always did. But the framed picture in front of the pulpit with a young picture of my boy proved that he wasn't coming back. There was screaming and shouting of people in the church as person after person got up to talk about Dave. They asked me to get up, but I told them I couldn't do it; I couldn't stand up in front of the church, speaking over his casket. Because of the gunshot to his head, there was a closed casket, which made it better for me. Seeing him unable to move would have drove me over the edge. In the front row was his family, and me and Momma sat a few rows back. Everybody was in tears as the choir sang one sad song after another. Through it all, I couldn't take my eyes off the brown casket with the gold trim. It could have been me in there, or maybe they could have had a double funeral. Two dead niggas dead over nothing, who'd accomplished nothing, and no one would miss them. I felt like shit sitting there, knowing that I'd had the power to stop Dave but I hadn't. I could have blocked the door or I could have tried harder to get the gun out of his hand. There were a million other things I could have done, but I didn't, and for that I felt like it should have been me laying there beside my friend. I thought about that all through the service until the pastor got up to preach. "Family, we aren't going to pretend here," he started "Brother David left this life in turmoil." I closed my eyes, listening and remembering those last moments. "But we don't have to live our lives in turmoil. There is something that we can do now before it's too late." I was listening as Momma squeezed my hand. I was tired of feeling like this and it seemed like every day things went wrong for me; I would fuck up or things would get turned around. Now my friend was dead: the only person I could talk to when shit went left was in a casket. "You can choose Jesus. He is the truth, and he died for your sins and you can choose him instead of the life you›re leading." I heard every word. I'd sat in churches before, hearing people talk about God and getting closer, but this was the first time I listened. "You've been going through it on your own. Every day is one pitfall after another and you have no direction." I felt like he was talking straight to me. "You don't have to keep going through that. God has a plan for you, but you won't find peace until you let him in." I listened to every word, looking over at my Momma as she cried, tears dripping down her face. "You can come up here now. We can turn this home going into a home saving." I looked from the pastor to the casket. "You can change, he can change you." The music started again, a low hum as he kept talking. "I know you›re tired. Because you've been doing it your way and it hasn't been working." I felt him; that was exactly what was happening to me. Every day, things I tried to do ended up like shit. "If you want a new life, come on up. Come here to the altar and lay it all on the line." I looked around to people waving their hands, but I wanted to get up. I wanted to lay it all on the line. I turned, whispering to my Momma. "I wanna go up." "Go baby, just go." She pushed me up. Standing, I felt like I was floating to the alter. Getting close to his casket, I couldn't stop crying. "Bring it to the altar, young brother." The pastor held out his hand as I knelt down, praying like I hadn't done in years. "Lord, today we come to you to help this young man." I felt hands on my shoulders and I couldn't hold it in. The tears were flowing like a river down my cheeks as I asked God for help. As a matter of fact, I'd never thanked God: I always cursed him. Mad that one thing after another didn't work, but maybe it wasn't supposed to work. "Lord, this young man has a calling on his life. Please help him walk in his calling and assist him in giving his life to you in the midst of this great loss." He said everything I was feeling. "Let the church say." Amen. I stood up on shaky legs, looking at Dave's family who was now standing behind me. Some kneeling next to me, but seeing his Mom made me weak. "You're my son now." She said through her quivering lips, sad and sick about losing Dave. "You go and be something for you and David." Her words touched me deep. I felt it all, and in that moment I felt like a new person. I felt Dave's spirit with me, as if I was living for him and me. Reaching my hand out to touch his casket, I gave my friend a promise. That I would live my life for us both. I meant it, and if it was the last thing I could do, I would honor Dave; because of him, my life was changed. He was more than my friend; he was a brother. And I wouldn't let him or his family down.

Chapter 24

The day after the funeral, I got the best news of my life. I wasn't HIV positive and everything was fine, but I still didn't feel right. I found out Beauty had left town; Dave's family had scared the shit out of her, threatening to kill her. I didn't have any comments on that... since the funeral, I wasn't even mad at her anymore. What was sadder was that for the rest of her life she would wake up and go to sleep with Dave in her thoughts, knowing that she'd played a part in him dying. After going up and giving my life to God at the funeral, I'd said I would ease into changing. That overnight I couldn't turn into Bible thumper, but I would try a little bit at a time to be better. Rapping always helped me feel better. But now, as I stood in the studio, my usual much needed therapy wasn't working. I spent two hours trying to lay down tracks, but it wasn't the same. I couldn't get a straight thought, Dave in my head and the whole situation making me feel sick. I wanted to do music: it was in my heart and soul, but since the funeral, I was changed. I couldn't talk about the same things anymore; I tried saying the raps I'd written before the shooting, but now that I was in the studio, it didn't work. "You wanna come out and hear it, bro?" My engineer said, his voice flat, unlike last time when he was rocking with the energy. I came out of the booth and he told me the truth. "I don't think you're feeling it, man." He was right. I rubbed the bandage on my head where my stitches were. "Let me just call it quits for the day, man." He nodded to that. I paid him and left, thinking of one person, Serena. I hadn't talked to her since the day in the hospital, but I couldn't get her off my mind. She was right, about everything, and I wanted to tell her, but before the funeral my pride had been in the way. But at the funeral, I'd learned something important. That in the grave we don't have any pride, knowledge, or the ability to be creative about anything. I had to do what was on my mind now. It scared the shit out of me to go to her, but I couldn't get it off my mind. I found my way to her house, sitting outside in my car and trying to figure out the words to tell her, but my heart told me I just needed to tell the truth. At her door, I knocked, promising myself I was just going to tell the truth. She came to the door and I let it all out. "Serena, I'm sorry." I apologized for everything I could think of. Some things that she didn't know about and others that she did. "I know that I don't deserve you, but I can't live without you." It was the truth. I was always too afraid to admit it because I thought being faithful to one woman was shit that punks did. You had to be whipped to do that, so I fucked as many women as I could. Thinking that I was something like a pimp, but I wasn't shit. "Landis, you hurt me so bad." She cried at the front door. I heard a voice that said 'marry her'. As I wiped her tears, I knew that was nobody but God. Momma said that the voice you hear is the Holy Spirit trying to lead you, or maybe it was Dave pushing me in the right direction. Either way, I was tired of running like some punk ass little boy. Now in front of the woman I loved, I wiped away her tears, telling her I was sorry, but now it was time for me to take it a step further. I slid down to one knee; no ring, just myself. "Serena. I know I hurt you and I'm beyond sorry. I don't have a ring for you, but I know right now I want you to be my wife." She was gasping, crying, shaking, but I just wanted to hear the words. I needed her to take me back. After losing so much, I couldn't lose another person, especially from being stupid. "But the AIDS...and the women..." "I'm negative, baby. And nobody else matters but you; I'm done with that. I promise. I gave my life to God at Dave's funeral. I'm done with it all." On my knees in front of the woman I loved, I prayed to God that she would give me the correct answer. "Yes..." she was crying, covering her face as I got up, squeezing onto her. I had a second chance at life, at my relationship with Serena, and with God, and I wasn't letting go. I knew now what my Momma had meant about being a man: it meant not being afraid to do what was right. I wasn't afraid anymore, as my cuffing days were over.

137

Epilogue

I would like to tell people that, after I proposed to Serena, that my life was peaches and cream. That we didn't have any other problems, but every believer knows that the closer you get to righteousness, the more the enemy tries to attack. It was an uphill battle for me getting a job, moving out of my Mother's house, and really becoming a man. A man of God and the man Serena and the children deserved. She had kids at home that needed a man in their lives, and when she gave birth to our daughter, that really opened my eyes. Plus, there were the children that I already had who needed me to grow up and be what God had destined for me. These last two years I've grown up so much that I don't sound anything like the Landis from a few years ago. I had strength that I didn't know about and it showed because I was doing the most difficult task to date. I was standing in the front of this church, preparing to take the hand of my bride. Watching as Serena walked in in all white to meet me at the altar was like a dream. I'd never thought this day would come: not just with her, but with anybody. If anyone had asked me two years ago, would I ever get married, the answer would have been 'definitely not'. But now in front of all of her family and mine, we were getting married. I looked at her as her step-dad walked her down the aisle. Thinking of how I'd apologized to the whole family for what I'd done. Until I found God, I didn't even understand how crazy I was or how reckless my attitude had been. But by the grace of God, they all forgave me. Her mom and her step-dad, and I even apologized to her cousin Tanya. Yeah, she came onto me, but I should have been a better man to stop it. The devil can use anybody at any given time, so I told her I forgave her and apologized for the part I had to play. Looking at all my family, my Momma in the front row holding our beautiful baby girl. We named her Davina, for my boy Dave. I missed him every day, and because of that, I didn't have a best man. I couldn't place nobody in his place. As Serena made it to my side, I felt like the luckiest man in the world. Tearing up as she took my hand and we stood in front of the pastor. I listened to every word and I couldn't wait until it was time for us to say our vows. I went first, ready to say the things to her and everyone else in the church. "Serena, love of my life. I want to apologize to you and thank you again for loving me through all of my faults." She was crying already. Fanning her face to keep the makeup from running. "I want you to know that I am a changed man and no one should have any thoughts about me. The Lord has changed me and made me new." I thought of all those changes. How I didn't even talk the same, or walk the same, and I darn sure didn't do the same things. I was now a gospel rapper, spitting bars for the Lord. A couple of years ago, I would have laughed if someone suggested that to me. "You are my everything and I will love and cherish you and our children." Her kids had become our kids. God really changed me because I didn't think this way before, and it had nothing to do with what she could do for me. Our family clapped and cooed, but I didn't do this for an award or for anybody's approval. The Lord put it on my heart, changing me into a man, and I knew I would serve him and take care of my wife until this was over. "With all of these things, I vow to take care of our family forever." I slid the ring on her finger with my shaking hands. I didn't have to cuff her anymore: she was my wife. Her kids were my kids and the child we'd had together was our child. She said her vows and I listened to every word. The old me would have been too anxious and impatient to even listen. But now I hung on her every syllable letting it sink in. This was my wife to be and these words would dictate our life together. But the most exciting part were the words I had been waiting to hear, the point of our whole ceremony. "With these words, I now pronounce you both man and wife." The pastor said giving us the greenlight. I couldn't see anybody but Serena. We kissed, the first kiss with the woman that God gave me. A man that findeth a good wife, findeth a good thing. That day in front of God and everyone who was there a became a man in that moment i decided that this beautiful woman was all I needed and she would never be an option because she was the only one 4 me.............

THE END

SNEAK PEEK AT TWISTED 2

ecap from TWISTED 1 After a long day, King wanted to do nothing more than go home and climb into bed. He decided to fix himself a sandwich and watch a little ESPN while he ate. After eating, King stripped down to his boxers and jumped into bed, pulling the covers fully over his head. He would deal with everything going on tomorrow; right now, he just needed a good night of sleep. The sudden feel of heavy pressure on his chest awoke King up from his sleep. His eyes popped wide open at the sight of his wife, straddled across his body, holding a gun to the middle of his forehand. "Baby wait," King screamed. He tried not to make any sudden moves to startle his wife and cause her to accidently pull the trigger on the gun she was holding to the middle of his forehead. "I trusted you," Mya sobbed, lightly brushing the tip of the gun against King's face. King could see the hurt, anger, and betrayal in his wife's eyes. Looking back, King wished he would have just been honest and upfront with his wife months ago. Mya laughed, "Imagine my surprise when I got home this morning to find this in the mailbox," she said, while hitting King across the face with a stack of pictures. King looked down when a few of the photos fell from Mya's hand, and landed on the bed. His mouth opened in shock, That devious bitch, he thought. In the photos, King's head was thrown back in pleasure, which explains how he didn't see the tramp taking the pictures. She had planned this all along. How had he let that sneaky bitch manipulate him into hurting the only woman he truly loved. Mya was his soulmate, his gift from God. "Mya, I love you baby," he gently said. Mya sat quietly as she looked down and stared into her husband's eyes. How had they gotten to this point? Just one year ago, they were saying "I Do" in front of their family and friends during a gorgeous wedding ceremony. The man she gave her virginity too, the man she vowed to love for better or for worse. King and Mya were supposed to be on a flight headed to Hawaii in just a few hours to celebrate their one-year anniversary. But that would never happen now. There would be no celebrations this year, or any other year for that matter. "If you really loved me, you wouldn't have put your dick in that nasty bitch," she screamed, just before pulling the trigger on the gun, filling the room with nothing but silence.

TWISTED
2

Chapter 1

KING AND MYA

King and Mya stared at each other in silence as feathers from the pillow Mya shot a hole through softly fluttered around the room. King shook his head a few times, trying to stop the loud ringing in his ears. "You're lucky I don't want to put Ms. Brenda through the pain of burying her only child," Mya said, as she threw the gun on the bed and walked over to the closet. Over the past year Mya had grown to love King's mother, Ms. Brenda as her own. King was his mother's sole provider and Mya knew she needed him.

That was the only thing that stopped Mya from putting a bullet through the middle of King's forehead. King sat quietly on the bed as Mya grabbed her luggage from the top shelf of the closet and began throwing her clothes inside. King knew he had fucked up and anything he said at that moment would only make their situation worse. He built his empire on the gritty streets of Detroit by having discipline and now wondered how he let himself be tricked into fucking his wife's best friend, Star. Mya zipped up her suitcase and walked over to their dresser. "I guess we're even now," she laughed, taking her wedding ring off and placing it on the dresser. "I'll send for the rest of my things later this week." With that, Mya turned and walked out the room. "Fuck!" King yelled out once she was gone. He looked down and noticed the envelope with the photos still sitting on the bed. King picked up the photos and slowly flipped through them. Star had managed to take the pictures from the perfect angle. The first picture showed her lips wrapped snugly around his piece while he gripped the back of head with his head thrown back in pleasure. In the second photo, Star was bent over the bed while King held her waist from behind plowing in and out of her. From the photos, it was obvious, King was enjoying every moment of their sex session. King ripped the pictures in half and threw them on the floor. He jumped off the bed and rushed over to the closet to grab an outfit to throw on. It was time he paid that bitch Star a visit. King tried to calm himself down on the ride over to Star's house. But the more he thought about the night that landed him in this situation, the angrier he became. Star sat in the corner of the bar and watched King as he took shot after shot, lost in his own thoughts. The women in the bar were like vultures and could smell when a man wasn't happy at home. King was a hood legend and women had no shame making it known they were willing to play any position he allowed them too, just to be a part of his team. Star laughed to herself as King waved off woman after woman that approached him. It would take more than just a fat ass to get a man like King, Star knew because she had been waving hers in his face for over a year now with no luck. After his tenth shot, the barmaid Maria cut off King's drinks. She was close friends with King's mother and had known King for his entire life. Maria refused to play a part in him having an accident on the way home because he was drunk. "That's enough big guy," she said, removing the empty shot glasses from in front of him. Marie knew something was bothering King because he wasn't his normal cheerful self but decided not to pry. Her main concern was him to make it home safely. Patting him on the hand, Marie told King to come back tomorrow and take care of his tab. She didn't want him pulling out a wad of money in the bar while he was tipsy. King stood up and kissed the older lady on the cheek. "I owe you!" He walked out of the bar and was thankful to feel the fresh air. He didn't realize how tipsy he was until he stood up. Making it to his car King dropped his keys while trying to unlock the door. A peep toe red bottom heel stepped on top of the keys as he bent down to pick them up. "You really shouldn't be driving in that condition," a voice said. King raised his head and came face to face with Star. He grunted in anger. "Move bitch," he said giving Star a shove to remove her feet off his keys. "You have turned my wife into a lying hoe just like you," he yelled. Star laughed on the inside. So, her plan had worked after all. King almost fell over when he bent down again to pick up his keys. "I'm not letting you drive like this," Star said snatching the keys off the ground before King could reach them. Hitting unlock on King's car doors, Star slid into the driver's seat. "Either get in or call an Uber," she told him while starting up the car. King already had a pending case and he didn't need to add a DUI to his list of charges. He walked around the car and jumped in the passenger seat. Star laughed at him sitting there sulking like a kid. Before they could pull out the parking lot King had nodded off to sleep. Mya drove quietly making sure not to wake him before they reached their destination. Twenty minutes later, Mya pulled up to the Embassy Suites in Dearborn and dashed in. She was happy to see King still knocked out in the front seat when she returned. King opened his eyes to the feel of someone lightly shaking him. He blinked his eyes a few times trying to remember how he had left the bar. "After what you said about Mya back at the bar, I didn't think you wanted to be driven home," Star innocently said while holding out the room card. She had to play her role perfectly if she wanted her plan to work. Snatching the key from her hand, King starting walking in the direction of the hotel room. The number of shots King had taken at the bar was pressing against his bladder. He didn't have time to stand outside and argue with Star. He would have locked Star out the hotel room, but she still had his car keys. When King emerged from the bathroom Star was sitting on the bed, with her jacket and shoes off. "Isn't it about time you go fuck somebody for your next meal?" he spat while grabbing the remote control off the dresser and flopping down on the bed. "I'm about too," she laughed. Standing up, Star slid the dress she was wearing over her head revealing her nude body underneath. The sight of her perky titties, wide hips, and plump ass had King instantly hard. King and Mya hadn't had sex in weeks. When Star saw the look of lust in his eyes she slowly walked over and stood in front of him. "You like what you see daddy?" she sexily said while caressing her nipples. Star leaned in and rubbed her perky titties across King's lips. The feel of King's lips against her skin sent an electric shock through her body causing her juices to run down her leg. King reached down in between Star's legs and roughly rubbed. He slightly moaned at the feel of how wet she was. King didn't know if it was the alcohol or his anger toward Mya that didn't make him stop. Star lowered her body to her knees and rubbed King's hardness through his jeans impressed with the size. She stuck her hands down in his jeans and lightly stroked him before pulling out his chocolate stick. Star's mouth watered at the beautiful, thick, long piece in front of her. She spit on it twice before taking it fully in her mouth. King's toes curled and mouth dropped wide open at the feel of Star's warm mouth. He watched in amazement as she switched from swallowing him whole, to licking up and down his shaft. King had been orally pleased by a lot of women, but none had ever given him a blow job this good. He now understood how she was able to pay all her high ass bills so easy. King grabbed Star by the hair and pushed her down further on him. The sound of her gagging and choking was turning him on. "Suck that dick," he barked. When King felt himself about to cum, he didn't bother to tell Star. He held her head still as he came down her throat. Star happily swallowed all King's seeds. King pulled his still hard dick from Star's mouth and yanked her up roughly by her hair. Bending her over the bed, he forcefully rammed inside her. King was surprised at how tight she felt after all the men she had been with. Star came the minute King slid inside her. She tried to keep her balance as her body shook from her orgasm and King pumping in and out of her at the same time. She made her ass clap and jiggle while throwing it back. King's loud grunts let Star know Mya wasn't putting it on him like she was. Star lost count of how many orgasms ripped through her body from the pounding King was putting on her pussy. He snatched Star's head back while roughly slapping her on the ass. The sight of his large red handprints on Star's huge yellow ass every time he smacked it, had him ready to cum again. King closed his eyes and got lost in Star's tightness and warmth. "Damn Mya," he yelled out as he came. When he opened his eyes, King saw Star, not Mya looking back at him smiling. King looked down in disgust, watching his semen drip out of her. "Get out," he spat. Star laughed as she slipped her dress back on. She had just got what she wanted, and maybe more. Star sat on her couch tipsy from the bottle of liquor she had been drinking all day. She tried to tune out the constant ringing of her doorbell, but whoever was at the door would not go away. Star stumbled over the half empty bottle of Cîroc as she stood up and headed toward the door. Star was so drunk, that she didn't care about being completely naked as she flung the door open and came face to face with King. The cold look in his eyes told Star that Mya had saw the pictures she sent in the mail. Before she could slam the door shut, King pushed his way inside the house and slammed the door behind him. Grabbing Star by the hair, he dragged her over to the couch and roughly shoved her down. "You are a jealous devious bitch," he roared, mushing Star upside the head. King raised his fist but immediately dropped it when an image of his mother popped into his head. No matter how mad he was at the moment, King could never bring himself to hitting a woman. Not even a bitch like Star, who deserved it. When King looked down and saw Star crying, he wondered how she could be the same cold-hearted person who hated her so called "best friend" to the point of trying to ruin her life. "I tried to warn Mya about you," King laughed while flopping down next to Star on the couch and picking up the half empty bottle of Cîroc off the floor. "I probably should have been warning myself," he laughed while taking a long swig out the bottle. King sat quietly on the couch and finished off the bottle of liquor, enjoying the buzz he was feeling. Anything was better than facing the reality that he had probably lost Mya forever. "Why?" King slurred as he turned to look at Star. That was a question Star couldn't really answer. She had been filled with hate for so long that she didn't know how to recognize genuine love. Star didn't hate Mya, she hated what Mya represented. Mya was confident, smart, and went after the things she wanted in life the right way. Those were all qualities Star didn't possess. She knew once Don found out what happened between her and King, they would be over. Just when things were looking up in Star's life everything began crashing down because of her own jealous actions. King noticed for the first time Star was sitting on the couch completely nude and couldn't fight off the lust that filled his body thinking of their last encounter. He tried to blame his desires on the liquor, but the truth was he was a man and like most men he was letting his "little head" instead of his big head think for him. King leaned over and began roughly kissing Star. He enjoyed the tart taste of alcohol on her breath as his tongue explored her mouth. When Star began kissing him back King knew there was no turning back. Star was surprised when King began kissing her and as much as she knew they were wrong for what they were doing she couldn't resist. Pulling her into his lap, King fondled and massaged her breasts. He gently squeezed her nipples before sucking on them one at a time. King reached under Star and pulled his hard manhood loose from his jogging pants. Star lifted her body up and slid down King's pole inch by inch. King placed his large hands on each side of her waist and guided her motions and she rotated her hips back and forth. "Damn," he grunted at the feel of her warmness. When Star's body began to vibrate from an orgasm, King exploded as well. Sweaty and out of breath, King pushed Star off him. "We can't do this again. We have to tell Don," he said. Shaking his head, King stuffed himself back into his pants and walked out the door. Star was poison and King had been bitten.

Chapter 2

MYA

Mya laid across the bed in her mother's guest bedroom and stared up at the ceiling in a daze. She didn't bother to turn her head and look in her mother's direction when she heard her walk into the room. Mya had spent the last two weeks hiding out at her mother's and refusing to talk to anyone. She felt betrayed and deceived in the worst way. True enough she had secretly aborted her and King's baby, but that was only because she thought King was cheating.

Mya honestly didn't feel like her actions justified King sleeping with her best friend. Looking back Mya had to admit she did overlook a lot of things about Star that she should not have. Star and Mya were best friend for years, yet Mya didn't truly know anything about her. Mya had never met any of Star's family and Star rarely talked about her past. Whenever Mya would try to bring up anything about Star's family, she would become angry and defensive. That should have been a red flag to Mya but because she truly loved Star, Mya ignored all the warning signs of Star's potential backstabbing ways. Mya's mother sat on the side of the bed and gently pulled her daughter into her arms. Mya let all her emotions out as she sobbed like a little girl. "Shh! Baby, it's okay," her mother said. "How could they do this to me?" Mya wailed. Mya's mother was not surprised at all by Star's behavior. She felt like Star was a snake from the first day she met her. But she was shocked, to say the least, by King. Her mother felt like it was more to the story and decided now was the time to figure out what happened. Mya's mother gently eased her daughter out of her arms and looked her in the eyes. "Did something happen that you're not telling me about?" she asked. When Mya looked down at the bed, her mother knew she was right. "I had an abortion without telling King I was pregnant. Mya's mother gasped in shock. "MYA!" she shrieked. She never thought her daughter would do something so cruel. She wanted to scold Mya but knew now wasn't the time. While she still didn't excuse the fact of King and Star sleeping together, at least now she had reasoning behind King's behavior. King was a man acting out of hurt. "Baby, one act of betrayal only leads to a thousand more. That was that man's child too. He had every right to be included in that decision," Mya's mother said in a voice full of disappointment. Mya sat quietly and listened to her mother's words. If she could turn back the hands of time, she would.

****

After staying with her mother for a few weeks, Mya was tired of the pity party. What was done was done. It was time for Mya to move on. She hadn't talked to King since the day she stormed out of their house, although he called her repeatedly. Mya wasn't ready to talk yet and probably wouldn't be ready anytime soon. She wasn't going to go as far as filing for a divorce from King, but she certainly wasn't going to go running right back. Mya brought home a nice six-figure income as a financial advisor and could easily afford a place on her own. She located a beautiful, small, three-bedroom brick condominium right outside the city and immediately fell in love. After a little negotiating, Mya wrote out a check to cover the full amount of her new home and handed it to the real estate agent. The real estate agent thanked Mya and headed out. Mya locked up her new home, jumped into her car and headed back to her mother's house. First thing tomorrow morning she would go pick out new furniture. "Out with the old and in with the new," Mya said out loud while searching though her Apple music selection on her phone looking for the perfect album to enjoy during her drive. She turned the volume of the radio all the way up when I Bet by Ciara came on. Singing along with the music, Mya couldn't stop the tears from falling down her face. I bet you start loving me as soon as I start loving someone else Somebody better than you And I know that it hurts, you know that it hurts your pride But you thought the grass was greener on the other side I bet you start loving me as soon as I start loving someone else Somebody better than you

Chapter 3

DON

Don sat on his patio smoking a cigar with a worried look on his face. He had been trying to get in touch with Star for over a week now with no luck. Scrolling through his phone and looking at their last text message Don was confused. He had just told Star that he loved her and was giving her the title as his wifey. Why would she just up and disappear on him? Don dialed Star's number again. When her voicemail picked for the millionth time, he hung up. Deciding to drive by Star's house, Don jumped up and grabbed his car keys before heading out the door. After driving by Star's house and not seeing her car outside Don decided to give Mya a call to see if she knew where Star could be. Normally Don would have called King first, but knowing how his partner felt about Star, Don felt he could get more accurate information from Mya, being that she was Star's best friend. Sitting in Star's driveway, Don rolled up a blunt of Kush before dialing Mya's number. He needed something to relax his mind. "Hello?" Mya curiously answered wondering why Don was calling her phone. "Hey sis, I'm trying to find Star. Do you have any idea where she may be?" Mya pulled the phone away from her ear like it had just bit her. Placing the phone back to her ear Mya asked, "Why the fuck would I know where that bitch is at?" Don dropped the blunt he was inhaling, just barely missing burning the Italian leather seats of the luxury car. Don was shocked to hear Mya cuss and even more surprised to hear her call Star out her name. Don brushed the ashes off his seat. "Am I missing something?" he asked confused. It hit Mya that Don didn't have a clue about everything going on. "Where are you?" Mya asked. "I'm sitting in Star's driveway." Mya told Don they needed to talk face to face and gave him her address. A million questions were going through Don's head. Why was Mya living in a different house than her and King's? Where the hell was King? Don hadn't tried to contact his boy since their meeting at the lawyer's office last week because he assumed King and Mya were in Hawaii celebrating their one-year anniversary, but now he knew that wasn't the case. But if King wasn't in Hawaii why hadn't he reached out to Don and let him know he was still in town. Don's body filled with dread as he started up his car. Something told him that he wasn't going to like the answers to all his questions. Don could have sworn he saw the blinds slightly move as he took one last look at Star's dark house before pulling off. "Maybe this weed has me tripping," he mumbled, while backing out of the driveway. ************************ Mya was unsure of why Don was looking for Star in the first place. From what she knew, the two could hardly stand each other. Suddenly, Mya laughed at that thought. There was a time that she thought King and Star could hardly stand each other as well. Mya went into her fully stocked pantry and grabbed a bottle of cognac for Don, and a bottle of wine for her. She already knew this was going to be a long night. Pouring herself a glass of wine, Mya got comfortable on the couch and turned on the latest episode of Love and Hip Hop while she waited on Don to arrive. It felt good to focus on someone else's drama for a change. Mya was just getting into the show when her doorbell rang. Turning the volume on the television down, Mya went to the door and let Don in. "Hey sis," Don said, bending down to give Mya a kiss on the cheek. Mya could tell by the look on Don's face he was nervous about what she had to say. Don followed Mya into the living room and noticed the bottle of cognac and a bottle of wine sitting on the coffee table. "That bad huh?" he lightly chuckled while pouring himself a double shot of the cognac.

"Unfortunately!" Mya sadly said, refilling her glass of wine. Mya grabbed her phone off the table and punched in her passcode. Mya scrolled through her photo gallery and stopped on the snapshots of King and Star that she was looking for. She handed her phone to Don; thankful she had thought to snap a few pictures of the photos and save them in her phone before confronting King with them. "What the fuck," Don screamed loud enough for Mya's neighbors to hear. "Is this some type of sick joke?" he whispered in disbelief. "I wish it was," Mya whispered. Don stared at the picture of Star bent over a bed in a hotel room with King sliding into her from behind. Don and King had been best friends since the sandbox. King was the only person Don trusted with his life. Never in a million years would Don have imagined King would betray him or Mya like this. At first Mya thought Don was in shock that King had betrayed her. But the more she looked into Don's eyes while he stared at the phone, Mya could see his hurt went much deeper. "Don, why were you looking for Star earlier?" Mya calmly asked.

Don hesitated before answering. Admitting why he was looking for Star, would be admitting that he had allowed himself to be deceived into thinking he could turn a hoe into a housewife. Mya's hands flew over her mouth. "You were fucking her, weren't you?" she screeched, slowly putting all the pieces of the puzzle together. When Don dropped his head into his hands Mya knew the answer to her question. "Did King know?" she wondered out loud. Don shook his head no. Pouring himself another shot, Don sat back on the couch and mentally went over everything he just learned. So, Star wasn't missing after all, she was hiding from him. Hiding from her deceit and betrayal. "So, what now?" he asked, looking over at Mya. When Mya began sobbing loudly, Don pulled her into his arms and gently stroked her hair. "It's going to be okay," he soothingly said. Mya laid in Don's arms enjoying the warm feeling of his arms wrapped around her body. Caught up in the moment, Mya reached up and placed a soft kiss on Don's lip. Don softly parted her lips with his tongue and hungrily explored the inside of her mouth.

As their tongues found a beautiful rhythm, Mya knew they had both just crossed a line there was no going back from. Don gently pushed Mya back on the couch and anxiously pulled the thin maxi dress she was wearing over her head. He gently sucked her hardened chocolate nipples causing her to moan out in delight. Don trailed kissed down her soft chocolate skin until he reached her neatly shaved peach. Placing one of Mya's legs on his shoulders, Don separated her lower lips with his tongue. He licked and sucked on her pearl causing Mya to squeal out in pure delight. Mya played with her nipples and became hypnotized looking at Don's deep waves on the top of his head as she watched his head move back and forth between her legs. "Shit," Mya hissed. Don was giving her the best head of her life. Because King had been Mya's first partner, she assumed everything he did in bed was the best, but that was because she had nothing to compare him with. The sensations Don's tongue was sending through her body caused Mya to realize how wrong she had been. When Don felt Mya's legs begin to quiver he tightened his grip on her hips. Her juices tasted so sweet he wanted to savor every drop. After two back to back powerful organisms Mya legs were completely numb. Mya laid in a state of bliss as Don stood up and pulled off his jeans and boxers. "Are you sure you want to do this?" he asked Mya while easing himself back down on top of her. When Mya reached down and grabbed his erection to guide him into her, that was all the answer he needed. Don slowly glided in and out of Mya enjoying the feel of her warmth. "Damn this shit good," Don moaned. He couldn't help but to wonder what would make King cheat on Mya with Star. Mya was the type of woman every man dreamed about. She had a good head on her shoulders and good pussy between her legs. What else could a man ask for? They both moaned out in pleasure as their pain of betrayal turned into passion. Don slowed his strokes and enjoyed the feel of Mya's soft lips against his skin as she nibbled and sucked on his neck. Don lifted Mya's thick legs in the air and plunged deep inside her. Mya's walls were so tight they felt like a vacuum around his manhood. Never losing his stroke Don placed Mya's freshly manicured toes into his mouth and gently sucked them one by one causing Mya's eyes to roll in the back of head. "Ohhhhhh... My... GGGGod," Mya stuttered as Don sent her body into convulsions. Don looked down and stared into Mya's beautiful eyes that were filled with pain and lust. Don felt his thighs tighten up as tingling sensations shot from his toes to his stomach. He wanted to pull out, but the warmth and tightness of Mya's walls had a hold on him. Grabbing Mya by the hips Don growled like an animal as he released himself deep into her. Don collapsed on top of Mya and they laid on the couch in an awkward silence for a few minutes before Mya jumped off the couch, grabbed her nightgown off the floor and ran into the bathroom. The reality of what she just did hit her like a ton of bricks, as Don's warm semen ran down her thigh. "Did I really just sleep with my husband's best friend?" For a moment Mya felt bad. "What goes around comes around," she smirked while turning on the warm water in the sink for a quick "hoe bath." Mya finished cleaning herself up and came out the bathroom where she found Don sitting on the couch staring off into space. Mya handed him a warm soapy washcloth to clean himself off. They looked at each other and both said, "This never happened," simultaneously.

About The Author

New York Times & International Best Selling Author Billie Dureyea Shell was born in Compton California and now lives in Ladera Heights with his wife and kids who he loves to spend time with. He is the Owner of several properties in the Los Angeles area and gives back to his community by providing low income housing to those who need it. He stated "It doesn't matter where you at or where you from it's what you do with your time. There's nothing you can't do if you put your mind to it".

Teri Woods Publishing
Presents

Family Or Not Some People
SCANDALOUS
Just Can't Be Trusted
A Novel

International Best Selling Author
Billie Dureyea Shell

Teri Woods Publishing
Presents
One Fake Friend Can Do More
TWISTED
Damage Than A Thousand Enemies
A Novel
New York Times Bestselling Author
Billie Dureyea Shell

Teri Woods Publishing

Presents

Don't Go To Sleep

New York Times Bestselling Author

Billie Dureyea Shell

TERI WOODS PUBLISHING
Presents

If you don't want to be stabbed in the back

BETRAYED

You should be careful who you let stand behind you

OPRAH'S
O
BOOK CLUB

NEW YORK TIMES BEST SELLING AUTHOR
BILLIE DUREYEA SHELL

TERI WOODS PUBLISHING
Presents

If you don't want to be stabbed in the back
BETRAYED
You should be careful who you let stand behind you
OPRAH'S
O
BOOK CLUB
NEW YORK TIMES BEST SELLING AUTHOR
BILLIE DUREYEA SHELL